EVE OF ERIDU

ALANAH ANDREWS

Michael Terence
Publishing

First published in paperback by
Michael Terence Publishing in 2018
www.mtp.agency

ISBN 9780648421108

I sat on the side of a mountain in Cambodia in 2017 and realised that the only person holding me back from writing a book was myself. I have had endless support from a whole bunch of wonderful people (you know who you are), but I think I really need to dedicate this book to my lovely grandparents in New Zealand. Love you!

www.alanahandrews.com

EVE OF ERIDU

ALANAH ANDREWS

Michael Terence
Publishing

I

'Take a seat.'

The chair looks like it belongs in one of those dentist surgeries from the stories of the *old world*, and I hesitate for a moment before crossing the sterile room. The synthetic material lining the back of the seat is cold, and I feel goosebumps prickle along my arms as I ease myself into the chair's rigid embrace. Up close, I note that there are thick straps attached to the armrests and the head support, and I glance sharply up at the medic.

'Nothing to worry about, Eve,' says Sia. 'The straps are just to hold you still while I complete the procedure.'

I nod, my jaw tight. 'Will it hurt?' My voice echoes strangely in the small room.

'A little. Nothing major. Why don't you tell me about your day while I prepare.'

My day... The events stretch out before me, a string of indeterminate length so that at first I can't work out where to begin.

Sia wheels a trolley over to the cupboard on the far side of the room and begins pulling out a number of metal instruments, arranging them on the top of the tray. I look away, focusing my attention instead on the cool, grey concrete below my feet. I don't need to see what she is preparing to do to me.

'What did you do this morning, Eve, when you woke up?'

The drink Sia gave me when I first arrived is already starting to take effect, and I feel reality blur slightly at the edges, the way it does first thing in the morning when your dreams collide with the waking world. If only I could pretend it was all a dream.

I see the jagged graph careening across the screen on the side of the illuminated tank. I remember peering into the opaque liquid and checking for any abnormalities. That's right…

'I went to the incubation chambers.'

Sia looks up from inspecting one of the sharp, metal tools. 'On your day off? Why?'

How am I supposed to explain the calming aura that saturates my mind whenever I am around those amniotic tanks? The way they are stacked together resembles the cells of beehives in the *old world*, and I always become readily absorbed in the data which tracks fluctuations in temperature, oxygen levels and nutrient delivery. Then there's the contents of the tanks themselves, suspended temporarily in a state of complete tranquillity. Whenever I am rostered on at the incubation chambers, I find myself gazing into the large vats of liquid, imagining that I, too, am so unaffected by the world around me.

But this morning there was no need to be at the incubation chambers – or any of my other regular duties – at all. So, how do I explain it to Sia? I can't, so I just shrug. 'It's the day of the harvest. I wanted to keep myself busy.'

Sia doesn't push the matter, and I close my eyes, recalling the wall of exo-wombs plunging into darkness as I turned off the lights. I remember standing in the darkened room for a few minutes, alone – except of course for the contents of the tanks – preparing myself for what was about to come. The gentle click of tools being placed on the trolley, combined with the effects of the drink, soothes me into a light slumber.

I am brought abruptly back into the present by the sound of the metal trolley being wheeled back across the room. The concrete floor is smooth, but the instruments clang together as the trolley wheels bump over the electrical cables running like arteries across the centre of the room, powering the machine squatting on a small table beside me.

'Sit back.'

I do as she commands, attempting to relax my body in the grip of the cold chair. Sia picks a pair of scissors up off the tray, and I can't help flinching as she brings them close to the back of my head. The monitor on my wrist glows a brighter, more intense shade of blue. Oh for founders' sake; get a grip, Eve. There is slight pressure and a snipping noise, and a moment later a chunk of long, dark hair spirals to the ground. I am being dissected; my shell is finally disintegrating, falling apart at the seams.

'And what did you do once you left the incubation chambers?'

Her voice is calm, soothing, and I appreciate that she is trying to keep me distracted from what is about to take place. I suppose she must perform these types of procedures all the time – when things go wrong.

'I went to the harvest ceremony.' I think for a moment. 'No, wait. First I went back to Block A.'

Sia returns the scissors to the trolley and they clink lightly against the other instruments. Then she picks up another tool, and I turn my head slightly to make out some sort of shaver.

She places a hand on the top of my skull, positioning my head so that I am facing forwards again. 'Tell me about it.'

The buzz of the device reverberates throughout my body and I clench my eyes tightly shut, bringing to mind the unit in Block A where I live with my brother and guardians. The room is small, with just enough space to fit two pods side by side, and a narrow walkway in the middle. My brother's pod sits below mine - eight feet of sleek white metal - and our guardians' pods cling to the wall opposite. Little dark plants cover most of the roof, as well as all of the available wall space; to generate the maximum number of oxy-creds, of course.

'I went to my room and lay in the base of my pod for a while, trying to read some of the set texts for the next cycle.'

Sia presses the shaver firmly against the back of my head. It pinches my skin slightly and I grit my teeth.

'Trying?' repeats Sia. 'You were worried, then? About the harvest?'

I know what she is hinting at – that perhaps there were already signs of what was about to happen. That I should have noticed and been prepared for the incident.

'No,' I say with certainty. 'My monitor was blue as always. I was just distracted.'

I recall practising my breathing and feeling the whoosh of blood pumping steadily through my veins, the blue glow of my monitor reflecting dully off the sides of my pod. No, there was never any hint of what was to occur. 'Luc was always at the top of the leaderboard, you see. There was no cause for concern.'

'Of course.'

The sound of the shaver ceases abruptly, and the room plunges into silence. I partially rouse from my memories but my body feels heavy, pulled down by the effects of the medicine. Reaching one hand up to the back of my head, I feel a small bald section and this brings me more fully back into the present.

'You've never felt any strong emotions before, then?' Sia replaces the tool on the tray and walks around so that she is standing directly before me. The question is unnecessary; she has access to all of my data on the machine beside her.

'Never.'

Her eyes are a deep blue colour, similar to my own, but I get the uncomfortable feeling that she doesn't blink enough and I avert my gaze. Sighing, Sia pulls the straps on the armrests over my forearms and fastens them tightly. I try to tell myself that I simply feel secure, and not trapped at all. It doesn't seem to be working, so I step outside my body and pretend that this isn't happening to me, but to somebody else, to another girl who went *old world* crazy and redlined this morning. It's not me. Not Eve. Eve would never lose control like that.

Detaching myself from the world around me is a strategy that has served me well in the past to cope with unpleasant events. Until this morning, of course.

'Tilt your head back.'

I relax into the seat and Sia does the straps up so that my head is pulled firmly against the headrest.

'What did you do once you left Block A?'

I watch as though I am a bystander, disconnected from what is occurring to the fragile shell pinned to the chair. After lunch… What did I do after lunch?

Oh.

How could I forget? It must be the effects of the drink, blurring my memories together and making the events of the morning easier to cope with.

'I went to the harvest ceremony.'

Sia attaches a pale, sticky pad to each of my temples, and I feel them adhere to my skin in an abstract way. Then she inserts two wires into each pad and connects them to the dark machine squatting beside me. I try to raise my hand to my temple, but of course I can't – my arms are firmly fastened to the chair.

My pulse begins to quicken, and Sia notices the way the monitor on my wrist is pulsing with more intensity. For founders' sake.

'Another drink?'

'Yes, please.'

She moves across the room to the small basin in the corner and fills a glass with water. I concentrate on every little movement that Sia makes; focusing on the minutiae helps me ignore the weightier thoughts that are pressing against my consciousness, insisting that I entertain them. She tears open another one of the little packets and the ripping sound is grating in the otherwise silent room. Pouring the contents of the sachet into the cup, she stirs it quickly with a spoon until the powder dissolves. The high-pitched *ting* of the spoon against the glass makes me grimace.

'You do understand why this procedure is important, don't you?' she asks, without looking at me.

I try to nod, but then remember the strap around my forehead, pinning me against the chair.

'I know.' My voice sounds strange, like it is coming from somebody else's mouth. I clear my throat. 'I understand why it is vital to have this operation. I am… thankful for the overseers' swift actions.'

I am well aware of what is at stake. If I don't have the memrase procedure then I am at risk of experiencing further unwanted emotions and plummeting to the bottom of the leaderboard. Like most teenagers in Eridu, I am willing to do just about anything to ensure that this doesn't occur.

Bringing the glass across to me, Sia holds it against my lips. The sickly smell of the liquid makes me a little nauseous, but I crave the release it offers. When she finally pulls the cup away, a numb sensation travels from my lips down into my stomach.

Sia picks something up from the tray but I can't see what it is from this position. Moving around behind me, she places a hand lightly on my shoulder.

'Tell me about the harvest.'

II

The format of the harvest ceremony was the same as always. In my mind, I see the screen descending from the ceiling of the auditorium and flickering into life. I remember the images of the past; pictures of war, and famine, and disease; all things that no longer exist. At least, not down here in Eridu. I have seen it all before, numerous times, and so I easily distanced myself from the grim history of humankind depicted before me.

'I spent most of it thinking about Luc.'

'Mmm, in what way?'

Something cool and wet is pressed against the skin on the back of my head, and an acrid smell fills my nostrils. I close my eyes and I can see the stage in front of me, flanked by dark blue curtains.

'Just wondering what he was thinking of. What he would be wearing.' I knew with almost complete certainty that my brother would emerge from behind the curtains dressed in the red of one of the premium positions. An overseer or an architect, that's what those at the top of the leaderboard were always harvested for.

When Sia slits the skin, I can feel only pressure. Thanks to the medicine, there is no sting of pain – just the sensation of my skin silently splitting apart, and something wet being mopped from the back of my head.

'So were you surprised when Luc wasn't harvested for a

premium occupation?'

I fall back into my body, remembering the way my monitor had pulsed with a bright blue light.

'A little.'

'Strong emotions are dangerous, Eve.'

'I know.' Of course, a little surprise wasn't the problem. A little surprise might cause your guardian to frown at you, but that was all. Unfortunately, this morning, for the first time in my life, I had felt more than just a little surprise.

When those harvested for the lesser positions had walked out onto the stage, my gaze had shifted from one face to the next, searching for my brother's strong jaw and furrowed brow. And then I had looked again, thinking that perhaps my eyes had jumped too quickly from one blue-clad figure to another. That maybe he was standing behind another student and I had simply missed him.

At first, I had felt only mild confusion.

But when Luc's name had appeared on the list of the culled, the confusion had turned into a different emotion; something deep and raw. The walls of the auditorium were closing in on me and I was falling down, down into the abyss. I had tried breathing deeply – *in for six, hold for six, out for six*, as I had been taught at the institute – but the oxygen pumps mustn't have been working at full capacity because I still felt like I needed more air. I tried to step outside my body, but for once I felt anchored to this shell of flesh and nerve endings. I had watched, helpless, as my monitor transitioned from blue, to amber, to crimson in less time than it takes to say 'infraction.'

It's fascinating, really, how emotions work; at least, it is once you are on the other side. From my classes, I knew about the increase in heart rate and blood pressure and the influx of hormones. But I never realised that experiencing a strong emotion could feel so physically painful as well. The professors didn't tell me about that part of it.

'I want you to think about your brother.'

I'm going to throw up. 'I don't think I want to do this.' I try to move, but I am firmly adhered to the chair. My heart thumps beneath my ribcage, and although I don't look at the monitor on my wrist I am certain of how it must appear.

'Calm down, Eve. This is for the best. You don't want to end up like your brother, do you?'

I stop struggling. She's right.

'Think about Luc.'

I bring him to the forefront of my mind. His dark hair and brown eyes, always looking so serious until he looked at me. The machine beside me whirrs to life and Sia inserts her flexi-screen into a holder in the base. It pulses with an array of different colours.

'Good, keep thinking of him, Eve. I want your strongest memory of him.'

My strongest memory… What would that be? Perhaps when we were young, walking along the tunnels that criss-cross Eridu and sharing our secrets. Or Luc tucking me into my pod at night, telling me stories of imaginary worlds with clouds, and wind, and rain.

'That's good, Eve. Keep him right there with you.'

I hear a small device turn on, making a high-pitched whine, and Sia's hand rests on my shoulder to steady herself, or perhaps it is meant to comfort me. I close my eyes. I feel numb. This is it, and I know it's for the best. No more Luc. No more memories means no more threat of feelings. To be content is to be free.

The instrument touches the back of my head and the whine

increases in pitch. My eyes prickle, and a single disobedient tear runs down my cheek. Of course, I can't wipe it away, and I taste the saltiness as it reaches the corner of my mouth and slips silently between my lips. When was the last time I cried? In my first few cycles at the institute, perhaps, when I was still unranked. Or maybe earlier, at the preschool, before I even received a monitor. There is no chance of it being more recent than that.

The vibration from the saw ricochets through my head and around my body, and I am thankful for the straps holding me still so the medic can do her job. This shell is not me, of course; not really. I know all about the distinction between body and essence, and I am well aware that the procedure is necessary if I wish to succeed in the next harvest. I try to relax and let the effects of the drink distort the whine and buzz of the small machine.

I sense, rather than hear, somebody else enter the room, and Sia pulls the saw away from my head. I open my eyes and see a blur of red. Strange. Red is not a common colour to see, except at the big events, and it makes no sense for an architect or an overseer to be here for such a routine procedure.

The sound of the saw cuts off, and then there is silence. I feel pressure on the back of my head, and then Sia walks around to where I can see her again. She peers into my face and I try to focus, but her features all blur together.

'I'm sorry, Eve,' she says, and the world stops spinning. I see her lips tighten. 'Equipment failure.'

At first, I think Sia is just going to get another tool – one that's working – but a moment later she loosens the straps around my head and arms. I want to tell her that she can't stop now; that after redlining once I'm worried that I'm going to do it again, tomorrow – when it really counts. My attempts to speak are thwarted by the inebriating effects of the medicine, and my mouth won't form the words. Perhaps she is just moving me to another room so that the surgery can continue. Perhaps there is a satisfactory explanation for why she is pulling the pads off my temples, leaving the thin skin tingling in the aftermath.

But if there is a reason, she doesn't tell me, and the edges of my vision grow dark. I try to talk again, but there is no use fighting the medicine, so I give up, surrendering completely as Sia helps me into a wheelchair. I settle into the seat and fall immediately into a murky oblivion.

III

Wheelchair. Guardians. Tunnels. Pod.

Each time I open my eyes I see another disjointed frame of my existence. I barely remember returning to Block A, climbing up into my sanctuary, and falling into a dreamless sleep. But I do remember the look that passed between my guardians when they realised that my memories were still intact.

I wake up early, well before I need to, and I stare at the inside wall of my pod. In the darkness, the lights on my monitor seem overly bright, and I tuck my hand beneath the coarse blanket, extinguishing the blue glow. If I don't move, my head doesn't hurt at all and I can almost pretend that yesterday was all a dream… That Luc wasn't culled, and that I never lost control. Cocooned in the darkness, I feel like a foetus suspended in the amniotic tanks at the incubation chambers; nothing can touch me here.

My mind wanders, and I allow myself to think. Not to feel, just to think. The training, the tests, the leaderboard – they were all supposed to prepare Luc for the harvest. So why was he culled? Nobody at the top of the leaderboard has ever failed the harvest before, that I know of. It doesn't make sense to me, but I take a deep breath, clearing my mind.

Remember your virtues, Eve, and have faith in the harvest. Being culled is no big deal, anyway. Separating the essence from the shell is a practice that has been taking place for many, many cycles. You just overreacted. Praise progress.

I ignore the prickling sensation that cascades along my arms.

I know that we have limited space in Eridu, and only the worthy shells can remain. After all, one day, when the radiation dissipates and a cure for the virus is found, we will inherit the surface and be entrusted with rebuilding humanity – the right way, this time.

But Luc *was* worthy, wasn't he? I push the thought away. Apparently not, and I need to trust in the founders and those who walk in their vision.

The digits on my monitor reach zero and my pod slowly fills with light.

'Good morning, Eve,' says the chirpy voice from my flexi-screen nestled in the small cavity in the top of the pod. 'Last night you slept for… Five hours, forty-five minutes. Your sleep quality was… poor. Recommended lifestyle change: Increase cardio exercise.'

Yawning, I reach up to prise the screen out of its hollow. It's not ideal, going into the first day of the cycle after a restless night, but there's not a lot I can do about it. Hell, it's not ideal to be going into my first day at the institute with my memories of redlining and the harvest still intact.

Unfolding my flexi-screen, I scroll across to my timetable for the day and scan through my subjects and after-school duties. I let out a breath I didn't realise I was holding; there's an appointment scheduled just before dinner with the medic, which must be my rescheduled procedure. I just need to keep myself under control for a single day, and by tomorrow I won't even remember that I had a brother. The thought evokes a strange, heavy feeling in my stomach, and I realise that I can't remember when I last ate.

Pushing the button that was nestled behind my flexi-screen, the pod cracks open to reveal the new day. On the other side of the room I can see my guardians' pods, still firmly closed, and I briefly wonder how they feel about one of their dependants being culled. On the outside they will appear content, of course, but I wonder if deep down – beneath layers of virtues and emotional barriers – they feel something. I run through the list of emotions in my mind. Confusion? Shame? Who am I kidding; my primary and secondary guardians are so well trained that they will merely feel satisfied that the appropriate outcome has been reached. It's in my best interests to feel the same way.

I climb down the ladder and walk across the unit into the small bathroom at the end of the room. Closing the door, I use a hand-held mirror to inspect the wound on the back of my head in the larger mirror attached to the wall. Even in this room, the walls are covered with the best oxygen-producing plants, although they are a different species than the ones in the main room. I learnt about them in my horticulture class; these ones thrive in damp environments which is why we are growing them in the bathroom.

In the mirror, I can see a small, square bald patch in the back of my head, with a red line extending through the centre. Prodding the area with my finger, I can feel the slightly painful raised section, but it is nothing too major; nothing that a couple of painkillers can't take care of. It must be covered with some sort of transparent dressing. Praise progress.

Sweeping my hair up into a ponytail, I am pleased to see that it will be easy enough to hide the bald patch, at least. It's unfortunate that I still have the memories of Luc, but I will just have to deal with it in the old fashioned way, the way people had to before the memrase procedure was invented. It's only for one day, anyway, and it's not like I've ever had issues with emotional control before – my ranking results demonstrate that – it was just a shock, that's all, to find out that Luc had been culled. I obviously hadn't prepared myself well enough. I am content, of course, with all that has happened. I'll just be a little more content once I can no longer remember it.

I peer into the mirror and wonder what the emotion was that I had felt the day before. I always imagined that strong emotions would have a distinctive taste; anger would taste like chilli and jealousy like drinking lime juice. Happiness; blueberries. Love; green beans. I suppose it's because at first we learnt about them in such an abstract way, through images and videos in the textbooks on our flexi-screens.

Anger: An emotion ranging from mild annoyance to intense rage.

I'd experienced annoyance, of course, but the concept of rage was so far out of my zone of experience that I could only watch the videos of people becoming red in the face and screaming and spit flying everywhere, and wonder vaguely how someone could react like that. How they could sacrifice their self-control so completely and become consumed by an emotion.

I could rattle off the physiological symptoms of course: increased heart rate; increased blood pressure; an influx of the hormones adrenaline and noradrenaline. But I never truly understood what it meant to lose control of myself so entirely, until yesterday.

And what emotion was that? It should have been sadness, I suppose. Sadness is the reaction to loss when someone has not embraced the virtue of contentment. But I checked the files, and the images of sadness include watery eyes and a downturned mouth. I'm not sure what emotion feels like physical pain in the stomach and an inability to breathe. Whatever it was, I don't ever want to feel it again. I shake my head, but stop quickly because it causes an instant headache. It doesn't matter what the emotion was, anyway; after tonight I won't even remember it.

I scrutinise my face in the mirror, but my eyes are dry and my mouth is arranged in its usual position. Good. I just need to keep them that way for one more day. I inspect the rest of my shell for any changes. After being the poster girl for emotional control, I feel like there should be some visible sign that I redlined. I peer into the mirror, searching for some newly created mark or expression that everyone can observe and deliberately avert their eyes from in the same way that those at the top of the leaderboard ignore the low-ranked. But my reflection gazes back at me in calm neutrality. I feel like it isn't really me, but the person I used to be before I redlined. I want to fall into the mirror and be that person again – and I will, soon, I just need to make it through until this afternoon.

I retrieve my flexi-screen from the pocket of my jumpsuit and flick across to the vitamin request form, perusing my options. Painkillers; Check. And something to help me focus after a restless night. I need to be at my best for the first day of the cycle. If I redline today, I won't get off so easily.

When I return to the main room, it takes me a full minute to work out what is bothering me. At first, it is just a niggling feeling in the back of my mind, like when you know that you wrote the incorrect answer to a maths problem but you can't quite figure out how to fix it. And so I stand alone in the centre of the room wondering why it feels like bugs from the Insectarium are crawling all over my skin.

And then I see it. Or rather, I don't see it, because it is the absence of something, rather than an object itself, that is amiss. In the area below my pod – where Luc's pod used to be firmly attached to the wall – is an empty space. I can see the bracket which used to hold it up, and there are no plants growing on this part of the wall, but other than that there is nothing to show that a fourth person used to reside in this room.

I tell myself I feel nothing. Sacrifice is a necessary stepping-stone on the path to success.

The pod was probably removed yesterday during the ceremony, but I was too disoriented when I returned home after my procedure to notice. *Failed* procedure, I correct myself. Of course, it makes sense that they took it away so quickly. After all, the culled have no use for pods anymore. There is a slight tightness in my chest, but I breathe deeply, as I have been trained. To be content is to be free.

Without any conscious thought, I walk towards the wall and stand in the empty space below my pod. I have to duck slightly, in order to fit, and I swear I can almost feel the traces of Luc's pod in the small space. When someone spends so much time in one place, perhaps they leave some sort of energy, a colourless residue that can still be felt if one knows where to go. It seems inconceivable that someone could just disappear with no trace left behind. I reach one hand over to the wall and touch the steel mounting bracket that remains there. It feels cool beneath my fingertips.

'Goodbye, Luc.'

The blue lights on my wrist monitor remain a calm, pale blue. Perfect.

And then I taste something salty and I raise a hand to my face. As I draw my fingers away, they feel wet, and I frown at the dampness on my hand. It must be sadness after all, but my monitor didn't register any change. Odd.

'Eve?'

I turn to see my secondary guardian sitting in the base of her pod.

'Are you alright?'

It's a loaded question, after yesterday, but I smile serenely and assure her that yes, I'm perfectly fine. I pull the sleeve of my jumpsuit up slightly to show her the pale blue monitor and she relaxes. I want to tell her that I'm going to be alright, that it's just for a day, just until the rescheduled procedure. The words stick in my throat.

'For the greater good,' I say instead.

She looks at me for a long moment before replying, but her face is expressionless as always.

'Rank well,' she says at last.

Happiness is fleeting and unsustainable. So many self-destructive decisions have been made in the pursuit of happiness. For this reason, in Eridu, the ultimate goal is not happiness, but contentment.

Book of Eridu

IV

As I enter the communal hall for breakfast, my eyes are automatically drawn to the large screen perched high on the back wall of the room. Of course, because it's the start of a new cycle it is devoid of the usual list of names and numbers, and I tear my focus away from the blank leaderboard. In a way, it is waiting too, as we are. It is in a state of suspended transition between one cycle and the next.

'Hi, Eve,' says the red-headed girl behind the counter as I scan my ID card. My eyes automatically gaze straight through her, as they tend to do with the low ranked.

'Hello, Hana,' I say, in a voice that I hope conveys my disinterest in talking to her.

'How are you?'

I look at her sharply, but it seems like an innocent question. After all, she has no way of knowing that I remember redlining, and that I still have the memories of Luc, for some inexplicable reason. At least until tonight. I could tell her the truth, of course, but that would be admitting that I remember everyone seeing me go *old world* crazy, and that's one memory that I'd rather forget. Besides, it would just prompt more questions; Hana isn't exactly the most disciplined of students.

'I'm fine.'

Hana smiles at me; and it looks like a true smile, not the mechanical grimace that most people wear on their lips without it ever reaching their eyes. No, Hana's light green eyes often seem to glisten with some emotion or another. That's why she's always near the bottom of the leaderboard. That's why we can't be friends. We used to play together, as pre-schoolers, and even sat together for a few cycles when we were unranked. Once our results had started counting, however, I'd had to abandon the friendship. Sacrifice is an important virtue if we wish to attain success.

'I'm going to do better this cycle,' she says. It's like she has read my thoughts.

'I know you will,' I reply, and I'd like to believe it. I've heard the professors mention that Hana's a bit slow, and hasn't realised that happiness is the trade-off you have to make if you wish to be successful. I think of the harvest, and of Luc. It's a lesson that we all learn sooner or later. Perhaps that day has come for her, or perhaps it will arrive at the end of the cycle when she is culled. My body feels unnaturally heavy for a moment, and I give myself a shake.

'I'll have a banana and some oats, thanks.'

The required oxy-creds are deducted from my family account and Hana hands me a tray filled with my breakfast and my morning dose of vitamins. I turn away and scan the room for a place to sit. Mealtimes in the communal hall are usually relaxed affairs. The young ones dressed in brown - the children who have not yet dedicated themselves to the virtues or are still unranked - giggle and play chasey around the tables. Their blue-clad guardians coax them back to their half-finished meals. Older children and teenagers sit in tight grey knots around the room, while their guardians congregate together in similar clumps. Brown, grey and blue jumpsuits; the colours mix together in the communal hall like a half-hearted replica of the rainbows from *before*.

'Eve!'

I look across and see my classmate, Lil, beckoning me over to a table where she is sitting with a group of other students.

Whereas Hana is the type of connection that was only plausible prior to being ranked, Lil is the ideal companion for me these days. At first she was lower down on the ladder, and we had little to do with each other. However, over the years, she began to excel at the tests and we ended up competing for first and second position over the last few cycles. My primary and secondary guardians both encouraged me to sever all ties with Hana and to associate with Lil instead, and I had listened to their advice. After all, I want to do well in the harvest.

I hesitate for a moment before walking over to Lil. Not that I'm seriously considering going elsewhere, of course, but because it is strange to see her sitting with a group. It's usually just the two of us, first and second, and I wonder briefly what has sparked the change.

As I make my way across the busy room I glance up at the leaderboard again, out of habit, half expecting to see my brother's name right at the top where it always sits. But of course, I will never see his name on the leaderboard again. His cycle is over, and it is time to move onto the next. It'll be *our* names up there soon. I feel as empty as the rows on the board. Get a grip, Eve.

I hardly know the other students that Lil is sitting with. A quick glance shows that I recognise their faces and can recall two or three names, but other than knowing that they all rank highly I don't really know anything else about them.

'Well, now that we are all here,' begins Lil, as I slide into the seat next to her. 'Congratulations on reaching the final cycle.'

I almost laugh, but quickly stop myself, appalled at the fragile grip over my emotions. What is wrong with me? Reaching the final cycle, however, is an event that hardly seems to warrant a need for praise. For the highly-ranked, it's a given that we will automatically progress from one cycle to the next. It's not so clear-cut for the low-ranked, of course, and that's why we learn not to see them. If you don't notice someone to start with, then it has less of an impact when they eventually disappear.

A girl whose name I recall as Polee leans forward and looks pointedly around the table at us all. 'Welcome to the elite.'

Oh. I pay more attention to the faces of the students that I am sitting with. Tara, Polee, and two boys from my biology class who I probably haven't exchanged ten words with throughout our time at the institute. Great. It must be because I'm tired that it took me so long to put two and two together.

'I thought we would have waited until the leaderboards were updated,' I say, and Polee frowns at me.

'Why wait?' She gestures towards her flexi-screen. 'We were the top six names when the last cycle ended, and I doubt that's going to change today.'

She's probably right - I hope that she's right - but I still can't see the rush. The others murmur in agreement with Polee so I decide I'd better not press the matter. Being in the top six is important, of course, but the only one of the elite that I could almost call my friend is Lil. I have very little interest in sitting with these other four students every day for the foreseeable future. Oh, get culled, Eve; sacrifice is an important virtue.

It's tradition, of course, and I remember Luc sitting at this exact same table during the last cycle with five other highly ranked students.

I'd like to forget how that turned out.

I'm starting to feel a bit sick, so I pick through the vitamins on my tray and find the two additional pills. Excellent, hopefully they will help me get through the day and I will finish at the top of the leaderboard as usual. Tomorrow, after the procedure, and after a good sleep, will be better I'm sure.

Picking at the oats in my bowl, I notice that Hana has finished her required breakfast duty, and is collecting her own tray of food. As she walks past us, she smiles and gives me a little wave. Silly girl. I don't smile back, but the others notice my glance.

'Do you want to go and sit with your low-ranked friend?' asks Tara, and although her face is impassive, and her tone even, I can hear the veiled sneer in her words.

'She's not my friend,' I say quickly, knowing that Hana can probably hear me. I hope that she doesn't react in any measurable way; I don't want to be responsible for her starting the cycle at the bottom of the leaderboard.

'Of course she's not,' says Lil, 'it's the final cycle.'

My stomach feels queasy and I have to force the spoonfuls of oats down my throat. I divert my attention dutifully back to the students I am sitting with. To them, the harvest has simply been the passing of time between one cycle and the next; a liminal space which holds no other importance than marking the resetting of the leaderboard. And, to be fair, that's all that it has meant to me up until now. But of course, I'd never had a brother in the harvest before.

'Soon our names will be up there, for everyone to see,' says Tara, addressing the screens with a vague wave of her hand. I keep my face blank and my monitor blue so that nobody can tell that I find the prospect a little daunting. Over the past few cycles, once we were old enough to be ranked, our names have only been visible on the leaderboards within our flexi-screens for the rest of the cohort - and our guardians - to see. But this cycle, our names won't solely be contained within our screens, but will also be projected on the walls of communal spaces for everyone else to view as well. It's motivational, or something like that.

I sit there in silence, letting the knowledge that I have reached my final cycle to sink in. That not only have I made it to the end, but that I'm also in the elite. For now, at least.

Not that it helped Luc at all.

For founders' sake, I'm starting to get a headache, and I hope that the pills kick in soon.

'Where are your duties this afternoon, Eve?'

I look up at Tara, barely registering what she is asking me. 'Oh, I'm at the preschool.'

'Lovely.'

She doesn't ask me about yesterday. Of course, they will all assume that the procedure was successful and that I don't even remember having a brother, let alone redlining. Going red at this age is unheard of, and I'm just lucky that it happened during the harvest, before the ranks started counting again. If there's ever a good time to redline, then I suppose yesterday was the ideal moment.

I can only wish that the procedure had gone ahead, because every time I think of Luc I become acutely aware of my meltdown. I have vivid recollections of the sensation of falling, of the walls closing in on me, of sucking heaving breaths into my lungs but feeling like the oxygen pumps weren't doing their job. How embarrassing, but at least everyone will pretend that it never happened. If I can't have the relief of forgetting the experience, then everyone else ignoring it is the next best thing. And by tomorrow, I won't recall the incident at all.

'Eve?' Lil touches me lightly on the arm, and I realise that I have zoned out.

What is wrong with me? I seriously don't cope well without a full night's sleep.

'Are you okay?' she asks.

'I'm fine,' I say, rolling up the left sleeve of my jumpsuit to reveal the monitor on my wrist. It is glowing a soft blue, like the pictures of the sky in the *old world* before the darkness came.

'Of course you are,' says Lil, carefully. 'I wasn't seriously implying otherwise.'

The others nod in agreement. Naturally, the girl who is regularly at the top of the leaderboard should be fine. I *am* fine. I'll be even more fine tomorrow. The elite tread carefully, unwilling for their thoughts to be misconstrued as criticism.

I finish off my breakfast, letting the conversation pass over me like the waves in the *old world*, and then I excuse myself. I have a full day ahead of me to prepare for. If I want to be at the top of the leaderboard I need to pay attention in class, ace every academic and physical test and socialise with the right people. Of course, I'm not concerned about those assessable areas. I feel a little fragile, and can only hope that the architects will be kind to us on the first day back and that there won't be any emotional tests until tomorrow. It's possible, but not very probable. It's more likely that they have spent the two days of the harvest planning the type of emotional assessment that will be sure to divide us all up cleanly on the first day. To separate the worthy from the unworthy. Great.

'See you at the institute,' says one of the boys. I search my mind for his name; Mat, I think.

'Rank well, Mat,' I say.

'Founders' speed.'

Book of Eridu

V

There are two pathways from Block A to the institute. The most direct route is through the perfectly straight A-Tunnel which emerges in a small courtyard at the front of the school. The second route is longer, meandering through a number of tunnels and cutting close to the outer wall before angling sharply back towards the institute.

I hesitate for a moment, but the longer route is paved with too many memories for me to be comfortable taking it today. No, after a sleepless night, my tenuous emotional control leaves a lot to be desired, and I'm not taking any chances.

I'm early, and A-Tunnel stretches out before me, dim and deserted. The fluorescent lights in the ceiling create little illuminated pools on the tunnel floor which envelop me as I walk along. It reminds me of the walls of the auditorium closing in on me yesterday, and I give myself a little shake.

It would have been wise to wait for the others, perhaps, to let their words fill my thoughts instead of this seemingly endless stretch of dark punctured with shards of pale light. But I wanted to be alone, didn't I, just for this morning.

The painted words stretching along the ceiling and creeping down the grey walls capture my gaze. Some of the other tunnels have images decorating their surfaces, but not A-Tunnel. No, the sides of this tunnel are adorned instead with words from the Book of Eridu. There are the commonly used phrases like, 'humanity with purpose,' and, 'for the greater good.' But there are some longer passages, as well, such as the section that opens the entire book. I don't even need to read the words as I walk past; I know them off by heart.

Do not rely on your own assumptions, but trust in the founders and those who walk in the light of their vision. It is only by surrendering completely to the will of our creators that we will be free.

'Praise the founders,' I say quietly, as I walk past the pale words. My voice echoes along the tunnel.

As the echo dissipates, I hear something else. Looking back over my shoulder, I expect to see somebody walking in the tunnel behind me, also on their way to the institute. But the tunnel stretches back, dark and void of all life. I've felt on edge all morning and this proves it; I need to get a hold of myself. I am Alexa, god of emotional restraint. Alexa wasn't a real god, of course, not really – although I suppose the founders are the closest things we have to gods anymore. The rest of them died when the bombs fell. Or did they simply give up on humanity when the virus was released, shaking their heads and choosing some other planet teeming with so-called intelligent life to bestow their wisdom upon? I can't remember what we were taught about the *old world* religions right now, but I suppose it doesn't really matter anyway. The gods are gone, that much is certain.

I'm only halfway through the tunnel so I pick up my pace and the words on the walls march steadily towards me.

The noise comes again, and I decide that it doesn't sound like footfalls after all. It is more like a low rumble, like an earthquake or a machine from the *old world*. I stop in the centre of the tunnel and listen. The concrete above me is thick and reinforced, but still, if there was a large enough earthquake…

The tunnel is silent.

No, wait, there is a faint sound coming from ahead of me. A regular *tap, tap*, like somebody rapping on the wall of the tunnel. I peer ahead, but there doesn't seem to be anything out of the ordinary. Of course, the little pools of light don't illuminate all of the edges along the tunnel.

There is nothing I can do but keep walking. The tapping gets louder, so I know that I am getting closer to *whatever-it-is*. I glance down at my monitor, but there is no reason to be concerned. And then, as I reach the place where I am certain I should come across whoever is tapping on the wall, something cold and wet drips onto my head. I step aside and look up, noting the thin, dark crack that splits the concrete above me. A steady drip of water is emerging from the crack, falling to the ground and making the tapping sound as it hits the concrete floor.

Tap, tap, tap. I look behind me, where another dripping sound has begun. Is there another crack? Has the earthquake split our home so that the water from above can enter? I back away from the water. If it really does come from the surface, then it will be contaminated with radiation and who knows what else.

Another tapping sound begins ahead of me, quicker, so that all around me now I can hear a *pitter-patter* of water leaking through the roof of the tunnel. My monitor begins to glow more brightly, but then I understand. How did it take me so long to work it out? This is a test.

I take a deep breath, and let go of my concerns. How stupid can I be? I knew that the architects wouldn't let us get through the first day without some sort of emotional trial. I suppose I just imagined they would wait until the school day started before springing it on us. It's smart, really, to shake things up and test us unexpectedly, a way to quickly divide the cohort up along the leaderboard. The final cycle is certainly going to be different than anything I've experienced before; a new level of testing in preparation for the harvest.

My monitor dulls to an acceptable level, and I walk deliberately along the tunnel. I keep my steps even, not too fast, and my head held high. The tapping sound turns into a hiss as the water courses down through the cracks and pools on the floor of the tunnel.

It's just a test, just a hallucination created by the architects to assess my emotional restraint. I've been coping just fine with them for years, and I'm pleased to see that my monitor remains blue. The water continues to fill the tunnel, rising up to my ankles, and then to my waist, and I have to admire how realistic the architects have made it this time. It takes effort, now, to walk along, and the undercurrent tugs at my feet, threatening to drag me under. It must be quite interesting, to be harvested as an architect, and to craft such hallucinations with the goal of making the participant *feel.* It's only a small part of their job, of course, but it must be the best part. I've always just wanted to be a preschool teacher, but perhaps I wouldn't mind being harvested for a premium position after all…

I reach the end of the tunnel and emerge out into the courtyard in front of the institute. Turning, I look back down the tunnel, but it's too dark to see if the vision remains. I touch the leg of my jumpsuit, but it is perfectly dry. It's amazing, really, the technology that our scientists have created to produce such hallucinations. Praise progress.

As I walk through the courtyard and enter the institute, I feel relieved that I have passed the first test of the day. After finding myself crying in the absence of Luc's pod this morning, I'd be lying if I said I was completely confident that I would be at the top of the leaderboard by the end of the day. I am a little frustrated, of course, that it took me so long to work out that the strange vision was a test, but I can't change that now.

I just need to get through one day, that's all, and then the procedure will set me right for the rest of the cycle. I will do whatever it takes to ensure that I pass the harvest.

Individual sacrifice must be embraced for the greater good.

Book of Eridu

VI

When I was very young, our history professor taught us about the heatwaves of the *old world*. I already knew what waves were, and so at first I had imagined heatwaves to be these giant searing towers of water, racing across the land and simultaneously drowning and scalding those who were unfortunate enough to stray into their path.

I was wrong, of course, about the nature of heatwaves, and my professor soon set me straight. I haven't thought about it for years, but for some reason the vision comes to me regularly throughout the day. Perhaps the morning test involving water cascading through the tunnel had triggered my memories.

What would I do, I wonder, if I knew that a wave twice the size of the tallest building was rushing towards me and there was nowhere to turn to save myself? Would I scream and cry and run, knowing there was no point? Or would I just sit down on the ground and accept my fate. Being raised in Eridu, the first isn't even an option.

The vitamins help me to focus somewhat, but as I sit at my desk, finishing the biology test at the end of the day, I have to admit that it seems to take more effort than usual to recall the answers, to type the correct words into my flexi-screen.

I feel peculiarly heavy, but I'm not sure if it's because of a lack of sleep, a side-effect of the pills, or if it's somehow related to Luc being culled. It's as though the gravity is just slightly stronger than usual, pinning me against the earth with more intensity than I have felt before. For founders' sake, Eve, there is no need to be so overdramatic. My appointment this afternoon can't come quickly enough.

It takes more effort than usual, but by the end of the school day, I am ranked in first position, as predicted. At least my duties at the preschool should take my mind off things until I head to my appointment.

While I enjoy working at the incubation chambers for their calming aura, being assigned at the preschool is just as pleasing for very different reasons. I'd be perfectly content to be harvested as a preschool teacher at the end of the cycle.

I check my thoughts. Of course, I'd be content in any position that I am harvested for. I have faith in the tests.

'Eve!' squeals the little girl as she runs over to throw her arms around me. 'It's so good to see you.' Most of the other children have already learnt how inappropriate such a gesture is, but not Tali. We aren't supposed to have favourites at the preschool, but she *is* pretty cute. The golden ringlets which fall almost to her waist make her look more angelic than she really is. I can only hope that she learns to control herself before she is old enough to be ranked.

I extricate myself carefully from her grasp. 'It's good to see you too, little one. How's everything been going?'

Tali screws up her nose which makes her look, somehow, even cuter. The five-year-old grabs me by the hand and leads me over to the small table and chairs where the children sit and colour in pictures on their flexi-screens. She sits down easily on the low chair. I, on the other hand, have to squeeze in, and even then my legs stick out the other side of the table. Tali giggles, and it is an unnerving sound. Soon, she will be taught to suppress such obvious expressions of emotion.

'Can you play with me for a while?' There is a flexi-screen on the table in front of her, displaying a half-coloured picture symbolising the virtue of contentment. In the image, a boy around my age is standing in front of the leaderboard with a totally blank expression on his face. I avert my eyes. It's silly, but for some reason he reminds me of Luc.

I open my own flexi-screen and click on the preschool tab on my timetable, scanning the requirements for the afternoon. 'Sure, I can play with you for a while. Are we going to do some colouring?'

Tali shakes her head vigorously, her little ringlets bouncing around in reckless abandon. 'We're going to play the Game of Virtues.'

She swipes sideways on her flexi-screen and the image disappears, replaced a moment later with the symbol for the six virtues. I smile; Game of Virtues was one of my favourite pastimes as a child as well, although there have certainly been some improvements to the software over the past few years. I navigate to the game on my own flexi-screen and we link our accounts.

'I'm getting a monitor soon,' says Tali, creating her avatar to have big blonde ringlets just like her.

'I know,' I reply. 'That's because you are a big girl.'

She smiles proudly, while I attempt to make my own character resemble myself. Long, dark hair swept back into a ponytail. Blue eyes. Medium build. Despite all of the individual features being accurate, the avatar encased within my screen doesn't really look anything like me at all. I am reminded of the moment of disconnection in my bathroom this morning; avatars and reflections are both imperfect copies of the truth. I quickly push the thought away. With a tap of a button, our characters appear on the screens, curled up fast asleep in their pods.

'Does it hurt?'

Tali's avatar wakes up and yawns, and a pop-up screen announces that she has slept for a full eight hours. Mine has only slept for five and is recommended an increase in exercise. Isn't that the truth.

'Does what hurt?'

'The monitor.'

Our characters eat breakfast and engage in small-talk, with various options for dialogue ranging from pleasant to downright rude. We make our selections and the characters level up.

'Not really,' I say. 'There's a slight pinch as the medics fit the bracelet to your wrist, but after that, you don't really notice it. It expands as you grow.'

Tali just looks at me doubtfully, reaching one chubby finger out to trace the edges of my own monitor which is glowing a pleasant blue. She watches, mesmerised, as the lights pulse methodically to the beat of my heart.

'What about the stim?' Her eyes fixate on the spot on my neck where a slightly raised bump is all that hints at something embedded beneath the skin.

I take a while to answer, pretending to concentrate on the game in front of me. I lead my character through a simple maths test and receive 100 per cent. The virtual leaderboard places my character at the top, with Tali just below me. *Great job!* announces the game.

'You won't get a stim straight away,' I explain, although I'm sure she already knows this. 'And once you do get one it's just a temporary stim for a few years - basically a sticky dot placed behind your ear. You don't get an implant until you're old enough to be ranked.'

Tali nods. 'What about the tests? Do they hurt?'

I think about the water rising in the tunnel. I can still feel the current tugging at my ankles.

'They don't hurt,' I say at last. 'But they feel real. At least, sometimes they do. If you practise really hard it gets easier to view them as some sort of dream.'

Tali frowns at me, her face crumpling in disbelief.

'You just need to remember that dreams, no matter how scary they are, can't hurt you. Once you realise that, then it's easier to cope with the tests.' I sound like my brother, and I become aware of the heaviness that still hasn't relinquished its grasp on my body.

'There's nothing to worry about, little one. And besides, when you first join the institute you will learn how to suppress easier emotions like excitement and passion. Those are quite enjoyable hallucinations, and you will slowly learn to control your body – and your mind – to ignore that type of stimuli.'

Tali nods, seemingly satisfied, and focuses her attention back on her flexi-screen, guiding her character through the story arc. Our characters are now old enough to be ranked, and we need to carefully consider each choice. After all, the game will be over sooner than expected if we are ranked near the bottom of the leaderboard at the end of any of the cycles. We've got to at least get to the harvest.

'You don't get to the harder simulations until you are older,' I continue, selecting the appropriate dialogue responses as my character interacts with her guardians.

I notice that Tali is clicking the responses without reading them carefully, which results in her score dropping dangerously low.

'Slow down-' I begin.

'Are you good at it?' asks Tali.

'Good at what? Game of Virtues?'

'No,' she says impatiently, her little ringlets bouncing in frustration. 'The tests. Your name's always at the top of the leaderboard so you must be really good.'

I don't tell her how hard I had to work this morning. 'Of course, but anyone can be good, it just takes practice. Listen to your teachers, listen to your guardians. I learnt a lot from my brother.'

When I mention Luc, I have the peculiar sensation of falling, but thankfully Tali doesn't pursue this line of thought. We reach the end of a cycle and her character is just above the cut-off line for being culled.

She leans in closer towards me. 'I've been trying really hard,' she confides in a low voice. 'But I can't help it.'

'Can't help what, Tali?' I say distractedly as I select my answers on a biology test.

'It's just that I really hate Tam.'

'Shhhh,' I say quietly, looking around to make sure that nobody has heard her. Tali's fierce little eyes glare at me.

'Are you gonna tell on me too?'

I am silent, trying to work out what I should say as Tali jabs her finger at her screen. Her character has succeeded — just — so far, but now we are nearing the harvest. The stakes are higher at the harvest, and more students will be culled. Don't I know it.

My character is still in the elite, and I scan through the options and choose the most appropriate response.

'You know I have to,' I say at last in a quiet voice. 'But you need to remember your virtues. I know it can be hard-'

'Why?'

'Well, it's easy to say something you shouldn't if you don't pause and think about it first.' I raise an eyebrow and gesture towards the options on Tali's screen, but she isn't making the connection.

'No, I mean why do I have to remember my virtues?' she asks.

Her character fails at the harvest and is sent to the Grid. *Game over*, announces Tali's screen. *You have been culled.* I sigh and put my own flexi-screen down on the table.

'You know why,' I say reproachfully, but Tali just sticks out her chin and shakes her head, her long hair swaying in protest.

She jabs a finger at her flexi-screen, exiting out of the game so that the announcement is replaced by the half-coloured boy in front of the leaderboard. I sigh again, but of course this is the purpose of working at the preschool, isn't it, to share our wisdom with the young ones – or something like that, anyway. I'm not sure that I feel particularly wise.

'We have to remember the virtues because that's how we are going to stop another darkness,' I explain slowly. 'If the superpowers in the 21st century had a rule book to live by, then perhaps the Third War wouldn't have happened.'

She doesn't meet my gaze.

'Hate is an unhelpful emotion, Tali. Restraint of feeling is necessary for a peaceful society.' I quote the words from the Book of Eridu, and feel pleased with the way they sound as they come out of my mouth. Perhaps I have some wisdom to share after all.

Tali looks at me now with doubtful eyes. 'But how does me hating Tam lead to a war?' Her screen sits on the table, abandoned.

'Think of it the other way. If nobody hates anybody else, then wars can't start, can they?'

Tali frowns. 'But isn't it a lie if I pretend I like him?'

I shake my head at her; this is an important lesson for the future. 'Not at all. A lie is saying you didn't break something when you did. This is just good manners.'

Tali is still frowning, but I think she understands. I will need to note down our conversation for the preschool teachers so they can follow up with her in future lessons.

She traces one finger along the edge of her flexi-screen. 'I heard my guardians say that Luc was killed.'

Thump, thump, thump, goes my heart.

And then her eyes widen and she puts one chubby hand over her mouth. 'I wasn't supposed to say that.'

'It's okay,' I say, and my monitor remains blue. 'But he was culled, not killed. It's different.'

She puts her hand down and screws up her nose instead. 'How?'

Thump, thump, thump. I stare at the content boy in the picture. He doesn't look so disinterested anymore, and I'm sure the edges of his lips are almost curled into an expression of smugness. But he can't really be smug, of course, that is an unhelpful emotion.

'If you are killed, you die. People died in the *old world*, but there's no death in Eridu. The founders took care of that.'

'So where is he then?'

How am I supposed to explain it? 'He doesn't have a physical form anymore,' I say at last.

'So he's dead.'

'No,' I say, a little more loudly than I intend to, and I look around to see if any of the teachers or volunteers heard me. 'No,' I repeat, quieter this time. 'You will learn all about it at the institute, but basically people are made of two parts – the physical shell that you can see and touch, and the real you, the essence, that's kept inside.' Are the pre-schoolers supposed to learn about this yet? Part of me feels like I've always known about the difference between my real self and my body, but I suppose I must have been taught it somewhere along the way. Of course, I only learnt about the specifics when working at the transfer centre.

'Well then, where's his… unphysical… form?'

'His essence,' I correct her. 'It's somewhere else.'

'On the surface?'

I shake my head. 'Nobody can really survive on the surface anymore, you know that. Not with the darkness, and the radiation and the virus. No, it's somewhere else. It's not here, and it's not on the surface – it's at a place in between. It's called the Grid.'

'So why are you sad?'

'I'm not.'

'You look sad.'

Kids.

'Maybe he'll come back,' she says.

'Maybe.'

'Do you think he'll come back?'

I sigh. 'I need to check on the babies so do you want to do some drawing with Kara while I'm gone?'

Tali nods, but as I walk away I hear her mutter under her breath, 'I'm still going to hate Tam, even if I don't say it out loud.'

Book of Eridu

VII

'Hey, Eve, guess what?'

I'm so close. I can see the door to the medic's office at the end of the Block A corridor, but I tear my eyes regretfully away from it and turn to face Hana. When I had noticed her walking towards me I had deliberately avoided eye contact, seeking to hurry past her without delay. Unfortunately, Hana has never been the sort of person to take a hint.

'What?' My voice comes out sharper than I intended.

'I'm not at the bottom. I mean, it's only the first day, but still. I'm really trying.'

I wonder if she didn't hear what I said this morning, about not being her friend, or if she just doesn't care. Perhaps she thought I was just saying it to save face in front of the elite. But surely she has noticed the way my gaze has passed straight through her body ever since we were old enough to be ranked. She was always near the bottom, narrowly avoiding being culled over the past few cycles, and I was always at the top. We aren't compatible and that's all there is to it.

'That's great, Hana, well done,' I say at last, hoping I can put an end to the conversation.

I should say something else, something knowledgeable about the virtues, but my mind is distracted. I can see the door to the medical room at the end of the hallway. My fingers itch to grip the doorknob and for my troubles to be over. I want to go back to feeling light and unburdened, to pass all the tests with ease rather than having to dedicate so much energy into simply recalling the correct answers from the depths of my fog-filled brain.

'How about you, Eve? How are you doing?'

I quickly stifle the feeling of irritation that seeks to flood my body. She knows how I am, my name is at the top of the giant screens plastered around every communal space. Every time she accesses her flexi-screen to read a textbook, answer a quiz, or check her timetable, my name is right there on the home screen.

'I'm fine.'

I go to walk past her, but she places one hand on my arm, stopping me in my tracks. I almost recoil from her touch; it's not usual to physically interact with another person, except perhaps in the preschool. It's not forbidden, exactly, but it is definitely discouraged because of the emotions the act implies.

Her voice is low and she speaks hurriedly, her green eyes searching out my own. 'You remember, don't you?'

Far out, what has prompted this? Was it something that I said? Did my face betray my concern this morning when she asked me how I was in the breakfast line?

'I don't know what you're talking about.' I try to keep walking, but she increases the pressure on my arm and raises an eyebrow.

'What happened? Was there a problem with the procedure? I'm so sorry about Luc. I was so surprised to find out that he had been culled.'

'Shhh.' I look around, but there is nobody near us to overhear her discontented thoughts. I don't know whether to continue the ruse or admit that I can remember and be done with it.

'Look, the procedure was postponed, okay. I'm heading to the medic right now to get it done.' I nod towards the door at the end of the corridor, the symbol for the six virtues plastered in the middle.

'But are you okay? When I saw you redline… Eve, I haven't seen anyone from our cohort redline in years.' Her eyes are filled with something. Compassion? I glance down at the monitor on her wrist, but it is still pulsating with a gentle blue light.

'I'm fine. I am content with all that has happened, and all that is yet to come.'

'Praise Alexa,' she intones. 'But Eve, why was he culled? Luc was always so good. He was right at the top of the leaderboard every single day, it doesn't make any sense.'

I don't have time for this. 'It's not our place to question what happened,' I say. 'It is our duty to accept it, and move on.'

'Have you moved on, then?'

I look at her, but it is as though I am standing outside myself watching the two of us together in the hallway, her right hand gripping my arm.

'In ten minutes,' I say, 'I will have.'

'Oh, Eve.'

Hana sighs, and for a moment her monitor flickers to amber. It is very quick, a mere millisecond, but I can't pretend that I didn't see it. Was it sadness, or regret, or one of the myriad other emotions that I probably don't even know the name for? It doesn't really matter which one it was; all strong emotions are forbidden. She lets go of my arm and I carefully step away from her. 'In the year of the harvest we must do all we can to rank highly,' I say.

Hana doesn't look me in the eyes. She understands. 'Of course. Praise the founders.'

'Praise the founders.'

I walk past her without a backwards glance, and rap quickly on the door of the medic's office before Hana tries to talk to me again.

'Come in,' calls Sia.

I enter the small room, closing the door behind me. I resist the urge to glance back along the corridor, to see if Hana is still standing there, watching me with regretful eyes as she remembers how things used to be.

'Eve, it's good to see you.' Sia gestures to a seat in front of her desk and I sit down. 'So, how do you feel?'

I really am sick of that question. She leans towards me slightly; her blue eyes are piercing, and I am reminded of my feeling that she doesn't blink enough.

'I'll be even better in a few minutes I'm sure.'

The silence stretches out before us. Perhaps it's the tiredness that makes it take me so long to recognise the look on her face. And then I realise why the appointment was held in Block A and not at the hospital. Oh. I'm not getting the procedure done after all.

My stomach clenches and it takes all my effort to remain calm. I open my mouth to ask, why can't I have the operation? Am I an unsuitable candidate? Am I too young? I'm sure I've heard of others getting the memrase procedure at this age. And then I close my mouth again. I am content. I breathe in for six, hold for six, out for six. Trust in the founders and those who walk in the light of their vision.

'It looks like you coped alright today.'

I want to tell her about the feeling of heaviness, but I don't know where to start. Instead, I push the grey sleeve of my jumpsuit up slightly and show her the pale blue of my monitor.

'Yes, I'm fine.'

It's not quite true, but I don't know how to describe what I'm feeling, anyway. Heaviness, emptiness aren't exactly emotions, at least none that I've heard of, and it's not like it's registering on my monitor. It's probably just a symptom of having a bad night's sleep, and I will be all better by tomorrow.

'Of course you're fine. I would have expected nothing less of you, Eve.'

I'm sure she would have said the same about Luc as he headed into the harvest. He is at the top of the leaderboard so he will be fine; I expect nothing less. I give myself a little mental shake.

'May I?' Sia gestures towards my head, and I turn slightly so that she has access to the wound. She removes my hair tie and prods experimentally at the back of my head. 'Much pain?'

'No. The medication helped.'

She hands the hair tie back to me and sits down.

'The incision is healing well, there are no complications at all.'

I just nod. No complications, except for the really important complication where I still have my memories intact. Breathe.

'I would like to apologise for the mix-up yesterday, and to assure you that it is beyond my control. But of course, you are strong. I know you will overcome this little incident.'

The statement that my cancelled procedure is beyond her control should allay my concerns; after all, we have been taught from a young age to be content with decisions and events that fall outside our personal influence. Today, though, the words are less comforting than usual. I want to ask her about the 'mix-up,' and find out why I couldn't have the procedure that would help me cope with Luc's disappearance. Was it something to do with the hint of red that I'm sure I glimpsed at the edges of my vision before Sia turned the saw off? The question sticks in my throat, and I know that she probably wouldn't answer me truthfully anyway. To be content is to be free.

Sia unfolds her flexi-screen and accesses my data. A horizontal blue line plateaus across the screen, with barely a hint of vertical movement.

'Impressive.' She scrolls to the left, revealing my data from the previous few weeks, months, and years. It's interesting to look at your life laid out like that, to see your worth represented in lines and colours and numbers. Aside from the red peak yesterday, my life resembles a horizontal blue stripe careening across the chart.

'So before yesterday, the last time you went red was…' she scans back through the data.

'Never.'

She whistles. 'You've clearly worked very hard to instil the virtues of Eridu.'

I want to tell her that she's right, and she partially is; I *have* worked hard to get to the top of the leaderboard. I pay attention in class, I do my homework, I study for tests… and yet some aspects of it have always seemed, well, easy. Luc was the same; he picked up the academic aspects of the institute with little effort, and I'm sure if I'd ever been shown his emotional chart it would have looked similar to my own. It was always so easy to do well, until yesterday of course. Yesterday caught me off guard, and now I find myself bracing for it to happen again, being ready to close my mind down and barricade the doors at the first hint of panic.

'Last night your sleep was interrupted.'

It isn't a question, but Sia seems to be waiting for a response, some sort of satisfactory explanation. 'Yes, it was the night before a new cycle; the final cycle. I know that isn't an excuse, but I was just thinking about today and that made it hard to sleep.' It's a partial truth.

'You weren't thinking about Luc?'

I keep my face perfectly blank. My monitor remains blue. 'No.'

It is odd, though, isn't it, what happened to Luc? Despite everybody expecting him to be harvested for a premium position, he had been culled. There is a queasy feeling in my stomach and I remember that I haven't had a chance to eat my afternoon tea yet. I hope that the appointment will be over soon.

'It's perfectly normal, you know, to think about him,' says Sia.

'I'm not thinking about him,' I lie. The overseers may have worked out how to keep track of our emotions, but they haven't yet devised a method for observing our thoughts. I think of the memrase procedure; perhaps being able to target specific memories is the first step towards creating such a technology. I feel cold. The overseers wouldn't want to do that though, would they?

'Thinking is not the problem,' continues Sia, 'it's only a problem if you start *feeling*.'

'I know,' I say. 'I'm not thinking *or* feeling.'

We sit there in silence, Sia looking at me closely as if she can tell that I'm not being entirely truthful with her. I leave my monitor in full view to demonstrate otherwise.

I know the deal. Emotions are dangerous. Emotions led us to the Third War. Restraint and contentment are important virtues for the progression of humanity. Praise the founders.

Sia sighs and sits back in her chair, tapping one finger contemplatively on the desk. 'And you will increase your cardio exercise this evening?'

I just want to go to sleep, but that doesn't seem like the most appropriate response. 'Yes, of course. I usually do twenty minutes on the treadmill, but I will increase it to thirty.'

'Make it forty.'

Great. 'Yes, of course.'

The medic shines a light into each of my eyes, tests my blood pressure, and extracts a small amount of blood for analysis. 'So you are sure that you feel nothing anymore? What's your view on your brother being culled?'

I shake my head. 'I have faith in the tests.'

She gazes at me for a moment and there is some odd look in her eye, but I can't quite work out what it is. Monitors are removed after the harvest so there is no way of telling if Sia is experiencing a strong emotion. It's not likely. By the time we reach the harvest, emotions have usually been drained out of us like the blood in her test tube. And if they haven't… I turn my mind away from that line of thought.

'Eve, it is imperative that you remain at the top of the leaderboard, and that you stay focused on the harvest.'

'I know - '

'There are things that I can do, to help you. Not that you need it, of course, but if you do…'

Now the heaviness and the queasy stomach are accompanied by the return of my headache. I wish I could just go up to my room, but I need to concentrate. 'What sort of things?'

She leans in towards me, uncomfortably close, and I resist the urge to move backwards in my chair. 'Well, the first thing we can do is provide you with some additional vitamins in your daily intake. Pills to help you cope if you feel at risk of something happening… again.'

'Sure, that sounds great.'

'Excellent, I will add the option on to your vitamin request form.' She types something into her flexi-screen and I feel myself relax slightly. Is it worth trying to ask her about the harvest?

'I do have a question though, if you don't mind,' I say.

'Of course.'

It's always risky, asking questions, as they could be viewed as breaking the virtue of contentment which would have an effect on my ranking. I decide that I have to try.

'My brother was always at the top of the leaderboard,' I begin, picking my words carefully. 'He went into the harvest confident that he would receive a premium occupation. He would never have imagined that there was a chance that he could be harvested for a lower occupation, let alone be culled.'

'I understand,' says Sia.

Was she surprised as well, I wonder, by the results of the harvest? Did she have complete confidence that Luc would be harvested for a premium position? Or could she tell, all along, the one thing that I couldn't?

I continue, carefully. 'I have always been at the top of my cohort's leaderboard as well. Now we are entering the final cycle, and I just…' I want to ask her why Luc was culled, what he could have possibly failed on. He had been so prepared and I feel myself falling. But no, I'm straying too close to showing discontentment; I need to demonstrate my faith in the tests. 'I just want to know what I can do to ensure that I don't go the same way as him,' I finish lamely.

'Of course,' says Sia. 'Eve, I'm sure that the harvest results were surprising for the architects as well. If Luc did so well at their tests, which are supposed to prepare students for the harvest, then they will be doing all that they can to work out what happened.' She leans uncomfortably close to me again, but I stay perfectly still. 'In the meantime, you keep doing what you're doing. And we will do everything within our power to ensure that you succeed.'

'I understand,' I say. 'Thank you.'

'Rank well.'

I rise to head out the door. 'Founders' speed.'

Idleness was a disease which infected much of humanity, and it spread quickly from one individual to the next. In Eridu, we must do better than our ancestors; to be productive and fruitful is important for a functioning world. We are a new wave of society — a strain of humanity guided by a sense of purpose.

Book of Eridu

VIII

Forty minutes of cardio. Great.

I scan my ID card on the way into the gym and scope out the available equipment. There are weightlifting machines, exercycles, and — my usual equipment of choice — treadmills. The gym is fairly busy at this time of the evening, but I spy a free treadmill in the corner and head over to it, weaving around an unranked boy with a skipping rope. Although it's true that exercising is low on my list of priorities, I have to admit that there are benefits to running until the sweat, the threat of emotions, and the memories pour out of you.

Before hopping onto the treadmill I place my flexi-screen into the groove at the front of the machine. It will automatically track the data on my monitor in terms of heart rate, distance travelled, and calories burned. The information is then used by our physical education teachers at the institute to help prepare us for the harvest.

I start off at a slow jog, in time with my heartbeat. I glance around the room but there are mostly low-ranked students around me, so I don't bother making eye contact. After a while, there's no time to think about anything else other than the pounding of my feet on the treadmill and the sweat dampening the back of my grey jumpsuit.

I would never voice it aloud, but I am usually fairly critical of running for no reason. Yes, perhaps one day we will return to the surface and have to run from whatever still exists up top; mutated animals that have adapted to survive in the darkness, the twisted dregs of humanity we call *masks*, and who knows what else. But down here in Eridu, it seems like more of a chore than a necessity. I understand that we need to stay physically fit in order to remain healthy, but the notion of constantly bettering my previous time or distance is one that has never really appealed to me, although I know that it is motivating to many of my peers.

Today, however, I find the run quite satisfying, and I continue to increase my speed until I'm sprinting along at a quick pace.

There is another benefit to being at the gym, I realise, one that I had never really thought that much about. Because the adrenaline released during exercise can produce a false emotional alert, for the twenty minutes – or forty minutes, as it is today – the readings won't count on my emotional chart. For the time being I can think, or feel whatever I want without concern for how it might affect my ranking. I'm not going to, of course, but it's nice not to have to concentrate so hard on clamping down on the threat of feeling.

My flexi-screen beeps to alert me when the forty minutes is over, and I step off the treadmill, slightly shaky; I've pushed myself harder than usual in the hopes of a full night of sleep this evening. I definitely don't want to start another day feeling so exhausted. The screen beeps a second time, reminding me that I'm due for my fortnightly dose of vitamin D.

I collect a towel and then head out into the locker room, stepping into the narrow tube-like machine in the corner. There is just enough room for me to stand in the centre of the tube without touching the sides. Scanning my ID card again, the transparent tube hums to life and I feel warmth emanating from unseen machinery beneath my feet, delivering a dose of vitamin D that will permeate my body, lasting for the next two weeks.

As I stand there bathing in heat and light, I notice someone watching me through the transparent wall of the sun tube – a boy with pale hair, about my age or slightly younger, is leaning against the wall of the locker room, staring at me. I don't immediately recognise him so I assume that he must be-low ranked, and I avert my eyes politely.

When I glance back towards him again, he is still watching me in an unnerving way. This time, I hold eye contact with him through the thin plastic, staring into his eyes which are so light they are almost grey. He doesn't look away, just smiles, and that's all the evidence I need to prove that he is low-ranked. I look down to check the screen in front of me, noting that I have thirty seconds left in the sun tube, and when I look back up he is gone. Insects crawl down my back, although I'm not sure why. There is a high-pitched beep and I exit the sun tube, refusing to waste my energy looking for the rude low-ranked boy. I have more important things to occupy my time, such as eating dinner and collapsing into a dreamless sleep.

***

The digits on my monitor flick to zero and the pod slowly fills with light.

'Good morning, Eve. Last night you slept for… four hours, twenty-nine minutes.'

I yawn, my mind filled with half-remembered dreams involving razor blades and leaderboards. I try to open my eyes but they refuse to obey my command. For the second night in a row,

I have tossed and turned and it feels like I only just got to sleep when it was time to wake up again.

'Recommended lifestyle changes: Increase cardio exercise.'

The voice is always so cheerful, and I pull the rough, regulation-issue blanket up over my head to block out the light and sound. More exercise? Is that the answer to everything? It's not like the last lot worked.

I doze off again, and a moment later a loud alarm ricochets through my pod. I jump, and my monitor flashes to amber. That's enough to wake me up fully. Far out, that's bound to have an effect on my ranking.

I retrieve my flexi-screen from the roof of the pod and push the button nestled behind it. The pod cracks open, the top half splitting along a hinge like a seed pod on the catalpa trees in the courtyard.

I scan over the timetable on my flexi-screen, yawning, and rub one hand over my tired face. When I draw my hand away, it is red and sticky.

'Shit.'

'Infraction recorded,' says the bright voice from my flexi-screen, as I cover my nose with one hand and awkwardly clamber down the ladder with the other. I'm not sure what is more shocking, the fact that I have a nosebleed or that I let the word out of my mouth. We all know the banned words, and occasionally think them, but to say one of them aloud is a slip-up I've never committed. It must be the tiredness; I need to be more careful.

I sit on the toilet with the cover down, head tilted forward, pinching the bridge of my nose and waiting for it to stop bleeding. I still feel strange, as though the girl in the mirror isn't me, but some imperfect reflection of the person I used to be. The person

I was before Luc was culled. Behind me, I can see the symbol for the six virtues reflected back at me in the dim light. The paint is fading, but the six triangles, their apexes converging in the centre, are clear as ever.

There is a quiet knock on the bathroom door.

'Eve, are you okay?'

It's my secondary guardian, and I wonder again how she is coping with the results of the harvest. Who am I kidding, my sec is as content as they come.

'I'm fine,' I call, and she leaves me alone.

'To be content is to be free,' I say to myself softly. The girl in the mirror doesn't look convinced. 'I am satisfied,' I begin again, with more feeling this time, 'with all that has happened and all that is yet to come.' A pair of dark blue eyes stare uncertainly back at me. I sigh, wiping my nose and throwing the bloody toilet paper into the bin. Leaning against the vanity, I lift the edges of my mouth in an imitation of a smile. 'Restraint of feeling, restraint of mind.' Much better.

I turn the shower tap on and step beneath the warm water, closing my eyes. I'd like to wash away more than just the remnants of the previous day at the institute and a few bizarre dreams. Scrubbing at my skin with more intensity than I need to, I imagine that I'm shedding memories and hints of emotional weakness along with my skin cells. Of course, I'd probably need to lose more than a few cells from my epidermis to go back to feeling like the person I was before the harvest.

I look down at my feet, watching the water swirl around them in little rivulets. Is this me? This vulnerable shell? But it's not, of course. The transfer system makes that very clear.

I gaze at the water slipping soundlessly down the drain. In the picture books from the *old world*, the water is blue. I'm not sure if it is some aspect of the filtration system, or the fact that we have recycled the water so many times, but the blueness has been completely stripped out of the water. The colour blue exists in our monitors — and a darker hue permeates the uniforms of most of the harvested adults — but water has been colourless for my entire life. Clear. Devoid of its previous lustre. When the blueness disappeared, was some sort of taste destroyed as well, I wonder?

I turn the tap off, thinking that perhaps that's what Eridu does; it takes something, like water, and strips it down to its basic components. Is that better, though, or worse? Maybe water used to taste awful, and now it is bland but drinkable.

Humans are like water. We used to feel emotions, but they were soon stripped away, just like the blueness, so that only the basics were left behind. I take a deep breath; emotions are dangerous, I *know* that, and so maybe blueness was too. It's probably better this way. Praise the founders.

The weight in my stomach is back again, so I quickly get changed and then head out into the main room to retrieve my flexi-screen from where I left it in my pod. Remembering what Sia told me yesterday, I flick across to the vitamin request form. This time, instead of just requesting the pills to assist with managing pain and improving my energy levels, I see a new option for an emotional control pill named Lortnok. Perfect.

I click the request button and fold my screen away. I'm determined not to finish the day in the same way that it has begun.

IX

'Eve, you're losing your winning streak,' says Polee, and I glance up at the large screens at the back of the room which have just been refreshed. Sure enough, my name is now in second position, just below Lil. I shrug.

'Perhaps I got one of the questions wrong on the biology test yesterday. I've got to give you lot a chance to catch up, don't I?' Of course, I know that my dip in ranking has little to do with my academic test results, and everything to do with going amber and swearing earlier this morning.

The elite all smile serenely as though the rankings don't really matter. As if it is of no consequence to them whether they are first, or sixth, or last. But the very fact that we are sitting together, despite the reality that we probably don't like each other all that much, is a testament to the fact that the leaderboard *does* indeed matter. And it will continue to play a significant role in our lives for the rest of the cycle, all the way to the harvest.

We eat our breakfast and I silently listen to the words of my peers wash over me. It strikes me for the first time that it is possible to speak a lot without really saying anything at all. I pick at my food, slowly spooning the thick gruel into my mouth without really tasting it.

Lil nudges me in the arm. 'You're awfully quiet this morning.'
'I didn't sleep well.'
'You need to increase your exercise.'

I just look at her, and then I smile and nod as though this is helpful advice. 'Thank you, I will.'

I watch as a man enters the hall from the door nearest the breakfast servers. Clad top to toe in black, the most unnerving thing about his outfit is the gas mask that he is wearing over his face, which transforms his eyes into two dark pits.

For founders' sake, how did a *mask* get into Eridu?

I could kick myself for jumping to such a ludicrous assumption. Of course he's not a *mask*. Since when did I become so irrational?

Masks are the small pockets of people who try to live on the surface, hidden away from the radiation in deep caves. They aren't immune to the airborne virus, not like the founders were, and so they have to wear gas masks in order to leave their sanctuaries. The *masks* have all been deformed from the fallout and die at a young age. This man doesn't look abnormal at all, so I know that I'm wrong. Besides, he's too well-dressed. Perhaps he's part of the military.

Some of the lower ranked students look up at the man as he passes by, but most remember their virtues and keep their eyes focused on their food. I mentally prepare myself, thinking that perhaps it will be another emotional test. I sort through my vitamins and find the Lortnok, the new addition to my assortment. It is purple and slightly larger than the other pills, and I put it in my mouth in preparation for what may or may not be about to occur. I crack the case between my teeth so that the sour taste floods my mouth – it will take effect more quickly this way – and then wash it down with a sip of water.

The soldier walks deliberately into the centre of the room and then turns slowly as though looking for someone. I think back to my lessons and realise that he's not military, after all; he's special forces. I doubt that he's real. I take a deep breath in through my nose and feel the pill start working. It begins in my belly, spreading a calm numbness up through my veins.

'Eve.'

'Yeah?' I realise belatedly that I haven't been paying any attention to the conversation going on around me.

'Lil was just asking what class you have first.'

I'm sure that I have already looked at my timetable today, but I can't seem to remember, so I reach one hand into the pocket of my grey jumpsuit and retrieve my flexi-screen. Unfolding it, the screen opens up to the size of a small plate and I flick across to my schedule for the day.

'Horticulture,' I reply, just as a loud cracking sound echoes around the hall. I look up as the soldier replaces the gun in his holster, turns briskly and leaves the room out of the same door from which he entered. I don't even need to step outside of my body. I am numb to it all.

I know what I'm going to see before I lay my eyes on her. A young girl – perhaps eleven or twelve, dressed in the brown of the unranked – is lying in a pool of red. I'm too far away to make out any of the details, but from the volume of blood gushing out of her, I imagine that it was a headshot. I dip my spoon into the bowl in front of me and dutifully eat my breakfast.

A boy sitting near the dead girl, also dressed in brown, captures my gaze. He clearly knows better than to make a fuss, but his eyes are wide and the monitor on his wrist shows that he is redlining. Someone sitting next to him - his primary guardian, perhaps – is unsuccessfully trying to calm him down. The monitor on his wrist is glowing a luminous crimson, far brighter than the pool of blood that is creeping ever so slowly closer to his feet.

I finish my breakfast, then turn my attention to the

leaderboard on the screens and wait.

Ten seconds pass. Twenty. Even the elite can't keep up their conversation now.

The board goes blank, and a moment later reappears with our new rankings. I smile serenely at Lil. A brief flicker of annoyance shows on her face, but is quickly replaced with a more appropriate expression.

She must have jumped slightly when the shot rang out, just a small reaction that would barely have registered as amber on her monitor. Or perhaps seeing the dead girl covered in blood had quickened her heart rate just enough to count as an emotional reaction. Either way, it doesn't matter; all that matters is that my name is now at the top of the leaderboard again and Lil has been pushed back down to second position. The elite congratulate me but I wave it away.

'It just takes practice.' I rise from my seat. 'See you at the institute.'

As I leave the hall, I make sure that I walk deliberately close to the dead girl's body, face blank, just in case the overseers are watching me.

X

Our world is predominantly made up of greys and blues, with a hint of red governing us all. Purple is a new colour to me, one that I've only seen in the little berries that adorn some of the plants around Eridu. It's fair to say that the Lortnok is the first purple object to be of any real consequence to me.

At first, it helps to make me feel almost normal again, like the girl reflected back at me in the mirror. I feel pleased about my reaction to this morning's test and optimistic about remaining at the top of the leaderboard throughout the cycle, even with the memories of Luc. By lunchtime, however, the pill is starting to wear off and the heaviness returns. Tomorrow I'd better ask for a second dose.

I am sitting with Lil at a table in the courtyard, eating my lunch and waiting for the others to arrive, when a boy who smiles too easily slips into the seat opposite me. I recognise him as the boy from the gym, the one who was watching me, and so I look straight through him.

The glare that Lil gives him should be enough to make anyone realise the error of their ways, but he seems impervious to her scowl. Instead, he reaches one hand across the table to me, and I raise an eyebrow.

'Sam,' he says, hand hanging in the air, waiting for me to take it. It's an archaic gesture, but I understand the meaning.

I gaze at him coolly and refuse to shake his hand. I know why he's here and I'm not about to give him a hand up the ladder.

'Eve,' I reply, although I'm not really sure why I bother responding to him.

'I know.'

Lil rolls her eyes. 'Well, this has all been a very nice introduction, but unless you're in the top six you shouldn't be sitting here.'

'I just wanted to speak with Eve for a moment.'

'Well, she doesn't want to speak to you.'

The boy, whose name I've already forgotten, looks at me, and I look down at my food. He doesn't seem to be at all disappointed, and the smile grows even wider. If I needed any more of an indication that the person opposite me was low-ranked, the ease with which he smiles is a damning indictment.

'Okay, well see you 'round.'

'I doubt it.'

Lil doesn't even wait until he is out of earshot before muttering, 'bloody climbers.'

I have to agree. Climbers – low-ranked students seeking a leg-up on the leaderboard – are becoming more and more common as the cycles continue. It's like they've finally realised the truth in the words that the professors have been telling us for years; that the harvest needs to be taken seriously. Of course, if they are only working that out in the final cycle, then it's a bit late anyway. Most of them try to set up a sort of mentor agreement, where a highly ranked student would agree to tutor a lower-ranked student in order to improve their ranking. There has to be some benefit for the high-ranked student, perhaps an exchange of oxy-creds or a desired vitamin that the other student has been prescribed. Of course, simply interacting with high-ranked students is enough sometimes to boost a score on the leaderboard by a few points.

Either the climber would have been trying to get me to impart some of my knowledge about the tests, or else he simply wanted to talk to me in order to get a few points on his social ranking. Either way, I'm not interested. Other than the low-ranked, the only other people who smile that frequently are those in the Grid.

The others arrive a moment later, slipping into the seats around the table.

'Eve had a climber,' says Lil.

'Oh, poor you. I had one this morning as well,' says Polee. 'Must be the day for it.'

The others nod in understanding.

'Shall we revise for the history test this afternoon?' asks Mat.

It's going to be an easy test on the politics of the *old world*. A revision test, really, to see what we remember from the last cycle. But I nod anyway because the Lortnok is wearing off and I don't want a repeat of yesterday.

'In which year did the Doomsday Clock reach midnight?' asks Tara, while I take a bite of my sandwich.

'Easy. 2075,' says Mat. It's his turn to ask a question, and he thinks for a moment. 'Who were the superpowers before the darkness fell?'

'Russia, USA, Germany, China, and India,' says Lil, counting them on her fingers.

'And North Korea,' suggests Mat.

'No,' says Lil, 'remember the incident in 2063?'

'Oh, right. Your turn.'

'Who released the first nuclear weapon?'

The questions and answers flow around the table, reminding me of the rising waters in the tunnel yesterday morning. I push the feeling down. I have no need to be concerned; it's just a basic test.

My flexi-screen beeps and I retrieve it from my pocket, glad for the distraction. There is an alert in the centre of the home screen.

Preschool duty: Cancelled. New assignment: Transfer Centre.

Well, that's just great. I place a finger on the alert and send it zipping off into oblivion. Lil raises an eyebrow at me.

'Change in duty,' I explain quietly, while the quiz continues on around us.

She nods, and I push the uneasiness back down to wherever it came from.

'Take a pill,' she suggests.

'I took it this morning already.'

'You might need to ask for an increase in dosage.'

I can sense that the others are beginning to listen in to our conversation, and I don't need anybody else to know about my irrational concerns.

'My turn,' I say, turning away from Lil and thinking about the types of questions likely to be on the test. 'Which nation was responsible for releasing the virus?'

On the day of the harvest each individual will be weighed against their scores and judged as worthy or unworthy. The worthy will continue our line of humanity, and the unworthy will be culled.

Book of Eridu

XI

Birth. Delivery. Dedication. Harvest. Pairing. Transfer. The six milestones in life dance around in my thoughts as I walk the short path towards the transfer centre. It is an honour, of course, to be present on the eve of that final stage. I only wish that I could still see it that way.

Before heading inside the building, I check the bushes growing on either side of the doorway for ripe berries, but the firmness of the flesh tells me they are still several weeks off. It's a shame, really; cracking through the soft shells and tasting the sweet juiciness of the berries is about the only thing I ever looked forward to when working at the transfer centre.

'Remember your virtues,' I intone as I enter the dome-shaped building – covered in little green plants like many of the structures in Eridu. It's been a long time since I was last rostered on at the transfer centre, and I'd started to think that the overseers had decided that it wasn't the right position for me after the harvest. Apparently I shouldn't have got my hopes up.

There is a scanner on the right side of the door as I enter, and I dutifully hold my ID card beneath it. There is a little beep, and then words appear on the small screen just above the scanner.

Scheduled Transfers: None

Praise Alexa. At least it doesn't matter so much that I took my pill earlier. There is also a note that I will be supervising the training of another student. Good; I'd rather not be alone in the transfer centre, even if there are no transfers scheduled.

I head into the back room which is lined with desks and small, silver, docking stations. Retrieving my flexi-screen from my pocket, I unfold it and place it into the slot in the top of one of the small machines and it instantly flickers to life.

Name: Eve
Task: Update transfer patch in Lot #3

At least it's an easy task today. I copy the section of code needed for the update, and then open up the folder marked Lot #3 and begin with the first file. Accessing the transfer file, I replace the code directly into the required sections, save it, and shut the file down. Then I need to test it to make sure there are no glitches. I activate the transfer file and the image of a man appears on my screen. The graphics software has clearly been updated since I was here last, and the approximation of a human face is more realistic than it has ever been.

'What's your name?' I ask, ignoring the usual formalities and pushing my unease away.

The computerised version of a human smiles broadly at me. 'You already know that, or else you wouldn't have been able to open my file.'

Oh, great, a cheeky one; just what I need. I'm sure that he would never have smiled that much in Eridu. Perhaps it's nice to be transferred and not have to worry about monitors and tests anymore.

'I've just updated the file and I need to make sure it's working correctly. So, if you don't mind, what's your name?'

'Trey.'

'Thanks, Trey. And when were you transferred?'

'7523 days ago.'

I should probably ask it some more questions, but I don't like the way its eyes are looking at me. The skin might look more natural now, but the eyes… the eyes shine just a little too brightly. The transfer centre gives me the creeps, even when there are no scheduled transfers. Besides, the patch seems to be working just fine.

'Okay, thanks for your time.'

The smiling face disappears, and for a while I work alone, immersed in the secret language of the computer system. I am just closing another file down when a slight movement out of the corner of my eye makes me jump, causing my monitor to transition to amber. Smooth, Eve. My heart hammers in my chest and, taking a deep breath, I command my monitor to return to its former, pale hue. What is happening? For years the required self-control has come naturally, and now I can't even seem to cope with basic day-to-day occurrences.

I compose myself, and then swivel around in my seat and immediately recognise the blonde hair, the light blue eyes that are so pale they are almost grey. It's the ladder climber; just my luck.

'Hello…' Oh for founders' sake, I've already forgotten his name.

'Sam,' he says, without a hint of annoyance, clearly understanding that if he isn't at the top of the leaderboard, then he is virtually invisible to me. Low-ranked students aren't usually assigned complex duties in places such as the transfer centre, but perhaps the overseers are trying to push him, to force him to step up and recognise his true potential.

'That's right,' I say. 'Sam. Well, take a seat.'

He sits next to me, in front of another docking station, tucking his hair behind his ears.

'So, how familiar are you with the transfer centre?' I ask, well aware that low-ranked students are generally only told the basics.

Sam reaches down into his bag and pulls out a book with a red cover. A real book, with real pages. I raise an eyebrow.

'I've started reading this, but I haven't got very far through yet.'

I recognise it as the Book of Eridu, but why he's reading it is anyone's guess. 'Where did you get that?'

'The library,' he says, as though it should be obvious.

The library, right. Luc used to take me to the library when I was little, to read me the *old world* books covered in dust, but I haven't been to the library in years. The overseers kept making it smaller and smaller, until it virtually became a cupboard within the institute.

It doesn't matter, though, because the professors distil what we need from the ancient text and upload it to our flexi-screens so there is no need to actually read the original volume, which is fairly disjointed anyway.

'You do realise everything from the Book that you need to know is on your flexi-screen, right?' I consider reminding him of the virtue of productivity and the need to wisely use our time, but I decide there's probably not a lot of point trying to educate someone who is low-ranked.

He shrugs. 'I thought I'd do it the old-fashioned way.'

'Yeah, okay, well you won't find much about the transfers in there anyway.'

He looks almost disappointed as he slips the book back into his bag. He is a bit slow, perhaps – one of the foetuses that didn't receive quite enough oxygen while in the tanks. That would explain the easy smile, the social faux pas this morning, and the look of disappointment which flickered on his face just a moment ago.

'I mean, you'll find the basic premise. Overcoming death and all of that.' I make sure that I speak slowly and clearly, in the hope that he understands, even if his neurons aren't working at full capacity. 'But the transfer system itself was invented much later. You do know that there's no death in Eridu, right?'

'Right.'

There's a look on his face that doesn't quite convince me. I glance down at his monitor but it is hidden beneath the sleeve of his jumpsuit. 'So the transfer centre is where the miracle happens,' I continue. 'Praise progress.'

He is silent.

'Praise progress,' I say again, but he just raises an eyebrow, his grey eyes almost mocking me. Definitely slow. I'll have my work cut out for me training him up in the system.

I clear my throat. 'Right, well since the dawn of humankind, there has been a flaw with the way people have been built.' I use the same words that Octavia used with me when I first went through the training. 'Specifically, the way that our consciousness is linked to our physical form, so that if the outer shell is irreparably damaged, the part of us that really counts also winks out of existence.'

Sam doesn't say anything, so I assume that he understands so far. That or I lost him back at the word, 'right.'

'When the founders built Eridu, they also built the Grid, so that when the body perishes our consciousness, our essence, has somewhere to go. When people elect to be transferred — or they are culled in the harvest — they come here and we complete the procedure, separating their intangible self from their physical form.'

I try not to think of Luc walking into the transfer centre after realising that he had failed the harvest. Did he wish he could say goodbye?

'Okay,' says Sam.

'Anyway, today we don't have any transfers scheduled, so we are just updating the system files.'

'System files?'

Perhaps he can only speak in one- or two-word sentences.

'Yes, see here?' I point to my flexi-screen which is displaying a large list of transfer files.

'But I thought it was a person's consciousness?' He looks at me, and it feels like a challenge. 'A soul, right? Souls have files?'

Hooray, he can speak in full sentences. 'Not exactly. Our essence is intangible, though, so when it goes to the Grid there is no way for others to communicate with you. That's what it was like at the beginning, when the founders first created the Grid. People just had to have faith that their essence lived on.'

'And now? Do you trap the souls?

I think of the presence I felt in the space beneath my pod.

'No. Trapped isn't the right word at all, and we don't call them souls.'

'Why not?'

I look at him, trying to ignore the sense of irritation that is threatening to bubble to the surface.

'We just don't.'

I get the sense that he already knows all this, that he is just goading me, trying to make me annoyed so that I go amber. After all, if I drop down the ladder, then there's room for others – for him – to move up. He probably saw me redline the other day and thinks I'm an easy target. I am determined to show him otherwise.

'The Grid is up there,' I say, pointing to the ceiling. 'And we can talk to those who have been transferred through a special program on our flexi-screens. Our job today is to update that program. As technology improves, we are able to update the system itself to better represent those who have been transferred. Got it?'

'So you've seen it, then? The Grid?'

We stare at each other. 'Not exactly.'

'So how do you know that it exists?'

I sigh. Doesn't he realise that it's rude to ask so many questions? I'm surprised that his flexi-screen hasn't announced by now that he has broken a virtue.

'Open up your book.'

He hesitates for a moment, before retrieving the Book of Eridu from his bag.

'It's right at the beginning, just after the passage about assumptions.'

Sam skims down the page. 'The founders saw that the world was doomed, and the fate of humanity as well. And so they dreamed of a new world, and they called it Eridu.' He looks up at me. 'Gee, they really liked to talk about themselves in third person.'

'That bit wasn't written by the founders, but by those who came after. Anyway, keep going.'

'The founders created Eridu deep within the earth, away from the sickness and the contamination destroying the surface. And above this, they built the Grid, so that those residing in Eridu may live forever.'

'See.'

'What, so just because it says so in the Book of Eridu, you believe it?'

I look around quickly, but Octavia is nowhere to be seen. He really needs to watch himself.

'Of course.' I can already see why he's low-ranked. 'The problem is, when people are sent to the Grid, the consciousness has no physical form, so we wouldn't be able to interact with them unless we use the transfer system. Does that make sense?'

'No.' Is he being serious, or just acting dumb?

'Think of it this way.' I look around for something to demonstrate with, but come up short. Instead, I put my hands together, one hand open around a fist. 'This is your body.' I show him the hand on the outside, the one that is encasing the other. 'The physical form that everyone sees.' Now I show him the other hand, the one in a fist. 'This is your consciousness. This is 'you' and the shell is simply the way you interact with others. Okay?'

He nods.

'We can now split your physical form from your consciousness.' I move the two hands apart. 'So you still exist, but you have no way of interacting with other people. You have no mouth, you see. If we don't use the computer system, then you just float around, you go to the Grid, and that's that.'

'Conscious forms, can't interact, go to the Grid. Got it.'

'When the founders first created the Grid, people just had to trust that their family members had been sent there. These days, we can actually interact with them. It's a miracle.' I try to keep my voice even.

'Sure.'

'The files, the transfer system… they are like the shell, like the physical body we use now to interact with others. By using the transfer system, we can interact with those on the Grid whenever we like.'

'With anyone?'

'Yes, with anyone.' I keep my voice light, but it occurs to me for the first time that I could actually speak to Luc if I wanted to. But I don't want to, not through the transfer system.

'It's a marvel, then.'

'It really is.' I nod encouragingly at him.

'So why don't you like it?'

The question catches me unexpectedly and I go cold. 'I don't know what you are talking about.'

His grey eyes looks directly into my own as he gestures towards my monitor. 'While you were talking about the transfer system, your monitor pulsed.'

'Nonsense.'

Did it, though? I'm sure that it didn't, and yet… Do I really have such tenuous control over my emotions that I reacted without knowing? No, I'm positive that I didn't have any sort of an emotional response.

'Anyway, well shall we get started?'

I turn back towards my screen, and a moment later Sam unfolds his own flexi-screen, places it on the docking station and accesses the transfer files.

'The patch is in here.' I tap on the appropriate folder and show him where to get the coding from. 'Then you need to drag it over here, open up one of the transfer files and insert the new code here,' I indicate a line of text, 'and here.' Sam is nodding, so I figure that I'm not going too fast for his oxygen-deprived brain.

'The final step is to test run the program, to make sure the new patch is working correctly. Simply click here and ask it a couple of questions. Its name. Family members. That sort of thing.'

Sam raises his eyebrows. 'It?'

I feel my cheeks get hot. Rookie error. 'Sorry. Him. Her. You know what I mean.'

He is still looking at me closely, and I have a sudden epiphany.

Perhaps I'm right in my assumption that he is trying to make me go amber in order to push me down the ladder. But there could be another reason for his interest, a much more chilling motivation. Either way, I need to be careful.

I watch Sam update the first two files to make sure he is doing the right thing. Then I return to my flexi-screen and we work together in silence.

I need to be on my best behaviour. I need a good score in the harvest.

I try not to think of that empty space below my pod back in Block A.

XII

'Did you talk to him about me?'

'What are you talking about? Who?'

I walk with Lil to her unit straight after dinner, one of the few times when I can get a private conversation in with her.

'Sam.'

Lil looks sideways at me. 'Who's Sam?'

'The low-ranked student, the ladder-climber who tried to sit with us yesterday. He was on duty at the transfer centre with me earlier.'

'Of course I wouldn't talk to him, I'm not going to jeopardise my ranking like that.' We reach the door to Lil's unit, and she turns in the hallway to face me. 'Why?'

I glance quickly up and down the hallway and lower my voice. 'He knew I didn't like the transfer centre. How would he know that, unless you told him?'

'Gee, I dunno, Eve. Maybe by your face.'

She opens the door to the unit and gestures for me to come in. I peer inside, but her guardians' pods are empty husks, lying open and vacant. I walk in and sit in the base of Lil's pod. Her unit is almost identical to my own, except that her pod is near the floor, not up high like mine. I try not to think about the fact that her pod is in the same position Luc's was in before it was removed. She doesn't have any siblings – most people don't – because the overseers are fairly strict about the guardians raising

74

one child at a time in order to provide them with the maximum amount of guidance. I'm not sure exactly how my own guardians ended up with two dependants, but I was never going to complain.

I make a face at Lil now. 'It's only around you that I let my guard drop a little, and never enough to affect the monitor. I was on my best behaviour, I swear. And besides, I wasn't even feeling creeped out today; we were just updating the files. Somebody must have told him.'

'Well, it wasn't me.'

'He said my monitor flashed.'

Lil turns to face me, concern lining her brow. 'Eve...'

'No, it didn't, I swear. I was being careful.'

Lil crosses the room and picks up the chair from beside her desk, moving it across so that she can sit in front of me.

'Eve, perhaps it did flash.'

'It didn't.' I have to work harder than usual to keep my voice even, and I suddenly feel very tired.

'Then how come you're in third position right now?'

I sigh. 'I went amber when Sam first walked in, I got a fright you see...'

Lil's face is expressionless, but her voice is soft. 'Eve, there's something I need to tell you. Something that might help you to understand a little about what you are going through.'

I just stare at her. She sighs, then looks at the floor.

'There was an incident. During the harvest. Nothing too important, however, you overreacted. You redlined.'

I wonder if I should tell her the truth, that I still have those memories of Luc. But it's not worth it. The incident was nothing too important anyway, according to her. Clearly, I just overreacted. After all, when your brother is culled, you are just supposed to get over it.

'I think,' she continues, slowly. 'That maybe the memrase procedure hasn't worked as efficiently as usual. You might need to book an appointment with the medic to get it looked at.'

I just nod.

'I'm serious. It would explain a few things, Eve. The fact that you were in second position this morning. That you went amber for no apparent reason. That you betrayed your dislike of the transfer centre…'

'I didn't feel anything – '

'Okay, Eve, so how did he know then?'

If Lil didn't tell Sam, then there's only one other person who knew about my aversion to the centre. I say nothing – I'm not supposed to remember him.

'I don't know.'

'And even if he did somehow work out that deep down – protected by layers of training and virtues and emotional shields – you didn't like the transfer centre, why would he bring it up? What's the purpose?'

'To throw me off the ladder, of course.'

Lil reaches into her pocket, pulling out her flexi-screen. 'What did you say his name was?'

'Sam.'

Lil reads through the first page of the leaderboard, examining each name in turn. Then she flicks through to the next page and does the same. She shakes her head.

'Eve, if he isn't on the first couple of dozen rungs, then bringing you down on the ladder isn't exactly going to benefit him.'

I'm inclined to agree, but I'm not ready to give up on that theory yet. It is a much more preferable option to the other possible explanation pressing against my mind. 'But what if he's going to use it to blackmail me?'

Lil folds the screen up and sits it on the pod next to me. 'In what way?'

'Well if he knows I don't like the transfer centre, perhaps he thinks he can use that, he can threaten to tell the overseers or something, in return for me mentoring him.'

Lil shrugs. 'The overseers probably already know about your aversion to the centre, anyway.' She gestures to the monitor on my wrist. 'They know everything.'

And if they do, then that just fits in perfectly with my other theory about Sam. The one that I'd desperately like to ignore. I feel sick.

Lil's flexi-screen beeps and she reaches over to check the alert.

'Sorry, Eve, I need to head to Polee's unit to work on an assignment. Do you want to come?'

I shake my head, mulling the awful theory over in my mind. It's a little far-fetched, but is it really completely unbelievable after all? I'm starting to get a headache, so I retrieve my flexi-screen and flick over to the vitamin request form. I click on the Lortnok and this time I make sure that I apply for a double dose.

In the old world, most people were free to choose their own partners. By the end of the 21ˢᵗ century, however, the divorce rate was up to seventy per cent. In Eridu, partnerships will be chosen based on logic and compatibility, rather than emotion.

Book of Eridu

XIII

When I return to my unit, my guardians' pods are thankfully vacant, so I sit at the desk and gaze at my flexi-screen. Making up my mind, I activate the transfer program. My finger hovers over the options, and I hesitate, wondering if I have enough courage to speak to the one person who could shatter everything.

I don't.

I push a different button, and a moment later there she is, my grand-guardian, framed within the edges of the screen. I almost close the program down instantly.

'Hi, Gran,' I say at last.

'Eve, it's so lovely to see you. It's been too long since we talked last.'

'I know, Gran. I've been busy.'

Thin lines lace her skin and I marvel at the clarity with which I can see her face. The recent update to the graphics card has definitely improved the visual aspects of the experience. It used to be clear that the image was simply a computerised rendition of my grand-guardian, similar to the avatar I created in the Game of Virtues; a stand-in shell to replace the physical form and act as a channel between Eridu and the Grid. Now, though, she almost looks real… except for the unnatural glint in the eyes. I think again that the programmers definitely need to work on the eyes.

'How are your sec and prime?' she asks.

'They're fine, Gran.'

'And school? Are you still at the top of the leaderboard?'

'Yeah, I am. It's the last cycle before the harvest.'

'Ah, the harvest.'

I want to ask her more about it, but I know what she will say. It's what all the transfers say when you ask them about the harvest. That there's a range of tests; physical, mental, emotional, and academic. That at the end you either remain in Eridu or you are culled. I decide to try anyway.

'What was it like when you were harvested, Gran?'

She looks up for a moment, as though thinking. 'Oh, it was a long time ago, Eve. I'm afraid I can't quite remember.'

I sigh. 'Well, what's it like in the Grid?'

Gran wasn't forcefully culled, as Luc was, but made the decision to transfer when she was 47. Young, old, premeditated, culled, we all end up in the same place eventually.

She chuckles. 'The Grid is wonderful, dear. Transferring is the best decision I ever made.'

I never met my grand-guardian before she transferred, but it's true that it seems to have been kind to her. My sec says she was never so friendly and talkative before the transfer. I should have no issues, and yet…

'I know, Gran. You always tell me that.'

Her mouth splits into a broad grin. 'Do I, dear? I'm getting forgetful in my old age.'

We both know it isn't true; she was 47 years old when she was transferred and 47 years old is how she will remain forever. We chat about schoolwork, and about my guardians. And then she says three words that make me feel sick.

'So, how's Luc?'

My body goes cold as soon as she mentions his name. I'm not

expecting it, and my monitor glows a little brighter for a moment.

'You should know, Gran,' I say carefully. 'Isn't he with you there in the Grid?'

'Is he, dear?' her voice trails off and I imagine her sifting through all the new arrivals at the Grid. What's it like up there, I wonder? Can you see who you want, whenever you want? Is it one big relaxing stretch into eternity?

'Well, so he is,' she says at last. 'It's a blessing you know, to have a brother. It's a bl-bl-bl-bl...'

The screen glitches and the image of my grand-guardian is stuck in a loop, repeating the same sound over and over and over. Her mouth opens and closes like a broken puppet, but her eyes… her eyes don't move at all. Without blinking, they stare out of the screen, still shining in an unnatural way.

It happens sometimes, and since Gran's transfer happened seventeen years ago, she isn't high on the priority list for updates.

In a way, I'm glad for an excuse to end the conversation, anyway. Clicking the exit button, my gran disappears from my screen to be replaced by the leaderboard. I consider selecting the function that will allow me to speak to Luc, but I'm certain that it isn't a good idea. If I'm fragile right now, I imagine how I might react if I were to actually talk to him.

If it really is him.

I check my thoughts. I need to stop being so critical of the transfer system.

I gaze at the leaderboard on the front of the screen and remember that I was going to search up the ladder climber's rank. Lil has already looked at the first two pages, so I start at the third. I scan through the names and then move on to the fourth, fifth and sixth pages, wondering how far down the ladder he will be. His name is nowhere to be seen. Perhaps he's going to be right at the bottom. I glance through each list of names until I get to the final page, but his name isn't there either. Odd. I must have flicked through too quickly. I scroll forward towards the first page again, going more slowly this time, checking the names carefully.

But something's wrong, and this time, I'm certain. Some ladder-climber. Sam's name isn't on the leaderboard at all.

XIV

I've always thought that it's pretty amazing what the founders achieved. To come from a world where violence was commonplace, where sickness and death and war were everyday terms, only to flip it on its head and create *this* instead. I look around the communal hall at our ordered lines and carefully chosen groupings. The only violence I've ever seen is contained within the educational films on my flexi-screen, and the fact that I will be provided with nourishing food each day is just a given.

Contentment may be a virtue, but it honestly shouldn't be that hard to remain satisfied when the entire system is based on crafting the best possible version of humanity. Coloured jumpsuits, ranks and tests, virtues and leaderboards… combined, they are all vital aspects to ensuring that every individual knows their place in this world.

So why wouldn't someone be on the leaderboard? It doesn't make any sense. Once you are old enough to be ranked, everyone is on the leaderboard until they reach the harvest. Unless…

I push the thought away; I shouldn't jump straight to the worst-case scenario. But I can't just keep my thoughts to myself, so when there is a lull in conversation at the breakfast table, I share my discovery about Sam with the elite.

'You probably scrolled too quickly, it's easy to miss a name on the board,' says Mat.

Of course it was foolish of me to expect surprise, or even a hint of curiosity from the elite.

'I checked twice,' I say tersely.

'Well, maybe he's so far down that the overseers thought it would be embarrassing for him to see his name on there.'

The others nod, but I'm not so sure. I play with the two little purple pills on the table in front of me.

'Well,' says Tara. 'What other reason might there be for not appearing on the leaderboard?'

'Faulty monitor?' says Polee.

'Perhaps.'

I look over at Lil but she is silent. Tara shrugs and changes the subject. The general consensus is that the low-ranked – or the non-ranked – are not worth our mental energy. I wonder if I should share my own speculations about why he might not be on the leaderboard, but I stop myself. If I tell them that, then they will know that I remember redlining. I don't think I can deal with that, not yet. Maybe not ever.

Anyway, the elite are right – the low-ranked aren't worth our thoughts. I gaze over at the table where Sam is sitting. He is reading the Book of Eridu again and I roll my eyes. Then I give myself a little shake. I need to take the advice of the elite and put him out of my mind.

But all day at the institute, the question of why he isn't on the leaderboard permeates my thoughts. I desperately want to come up with a reasonable answer that doesn't make my skin crawl.

I'm sitting in history class, gazing at the back of Sam's head when I decide to tackle the situation rationally. Professor Cattaro's voice is droning on about the politics of before, and I retrieve an old notebook from my bag. Under the guise of taking notes the old-fashioned way, I draw up two columns on a single page. Logic; that's all I need to sort this out.

I label the first column 'ladder climber,' and the second 'informer.' Are there any other possibilities for who he might be? I stare at the pale hair on the back of his head and decide I may as well write down all of my ideas, even the far-fetched ones.

Turning to a new page, I draw up three columns this time. I strain my mind, trying to work out if I had ever noticed Sam at the institute before I saw him staring at me in the gym. It's no use. Looking around at the other low-ranked students, there are only a handful that I can identify by name, and perhaps another half-dozen who I recognise, but can't say for sure who they are. Then there's the rest of them, stretching out before me in the large classroom, identical in their grey jumpsuits and low ranking. Still, that's enough to add another heading to my columns.

Beside 'ladder climber,' and 'informer,' I now add '*mask.*' It's impossible, of course, but it's important to entertain all options.

As Professor Cattaro describes the different political systems of the *old world,* I add my evidence beneath each heading.

The notes under 'ladder climber,' are the easiest to write. After all, that's the primary reason why anyone outside of the top six would want to interact with me, to get a boost in their social ranking. There are other pieces of evidence that fit in with his hypothesis too; the ease with which he smiles, the way he accused me of *feeling* at the transfer centre. Some low-ranked students are at the bottom because of their academic or physical test results, but many struggle with emotional control instead. He must have seen me redline during the harvest and thought I was an easy target. I can't forget the way he was watching me at the gym.

He probably already talked to Luc through the transfer system and somehow got him to share my one weakness; my aversion to the transfer centre. Then it was simple — say whatever he could to make me feel an emotion. The further I fall, the easier he can climb. There is only one problem with this hypothesis; the fact that I couldn't find his name on the leaderboard. If he's not on the leaderboard, then he can't exactly be a ladder climber, can he? Perhaps I really did just scroll too fast, or Polee is right about his monitor being broken.

The evidence under the next heading, 'informer,' also comes more easily than I would have liked.

I roll my pencil between my fingers and prod my thoughts this way and that. This is the hypothesis that I'd really like to be inaccurate, but I can't ignore the possibility. I heard Luc speak about rumours of informers in his last cycle, and it's certainly not impossible for Sam to be one.

I know that most of our harvest scores are decided by our performance in tests, but some attributes aren't assessable in that way. Physics, history, biology, chemistry, emotional control, fitness – our competence in all of these areas is easily condensed into a single score based on a series of exams. But what about leadership? What about collaboration? Or patriotism? I know that these elements are assessed not from exams, but from our teachers' observations over the past seventeen years. Even as a preschool volunteer I am required to report back on the children I work with. But our teachers and our guardians can't be around us all the time.

And now that I've redlined once, the overseers are probably checking up on me, seeing if I'm upholding the virtues. Maybe that's what happened to Luc, he redlined in the final test. Or perhaps Sam's not here specifically to watch *me*, but to watch all of us. If he is working for the overseers then it answers why he isn't on the leaderboard; either he is a young-looking adult who has been asked to pose as a student, or the overseers have cut him a deal with his ranking. After all, most virtuous students wouldn't actively seek out Sam's rank or try to work out why he wasn't on the leaderboard. They would simply be content that the overseers are taking care of it. I move onto the final column. I suppose I'm not the virtuous student I always imagined myself to be.

The main piece of evidence for Sam being a *mask* is that he isn't on the leaderboard. That, and that I can't remember having seen him at the institute before yesterday – not that this means much. *Masks* aren't simply fantasy stories, though, as much as I'd like to imagine that the deformed dregs of humankind attempting to survive in deep caves and mines are a product of someone's twisted imagination. They aren't immune, of course, to the virus, and so if they leave their dark hovels for any reason they must wear an oxygen mask in an attempt to avoid contracting the disease that crawls on the surface of the earth. Hence their name; *masks*. What they can't avoid, however, is the radiation which seeps into their very DNA, causing birth defects, hideous deformities, and early death.

Gazing at the back of Sam's perfectly formed skull, it's difficult to entertain such a thought, and yet it is still preferable to him being an informer, *and* it answers why he isn't on the leaderboard. Why would the overseers accept a *mask* into Eridu, though?

I glance over at Lil, but she is dutifully copying notes into her flexi-screen. Was her silence this morning a symptom of not caring, or was it something else? Does she harbour the same thoughts that I do? I turn to a blank page and place the point of my pencil against the paper, working out what to write. I know that I should just leave it, but now that I have set my thoughts into motion they are gaining momentum.

I write a question in the centre of the page, tearing it carefully, silently, out of my book, and then I wait for an opportune moment to slide it across the desk to Lil. Professor Cattaro's strict classroom manner has only intensified with age, and I know that if he catches me writing notes, I will likely lose my leisure time for the day - if not two.

I am willing to risk it. As the professor looks down to sketch the structure of 21st Century society onto his display so that it appears on the wall behind him, I covertly slide the note across the desk to Lil. She frowns, but compliantly places a hand over the note and slides it out of sight.

At that moment, Professor Cattaro stares directly at me, and I focus all of my attention into keeping my face impassive. My monitor is calmly pulsating with a blue light and I plan on keeping it that way. Taking a deep breath, I duck my head and write down the names of the superpowers before the darkness came.

Out of the corner of my eye, I can see Lil reading my note under the desk, and then begin scrawling something back. I silently beg her not to pass the note back to me, not yet. Professor Cattaro is busy describing the impacts of global warming but I notice his eyes rest on me far too often – he knows I am up to something. Then, as he circles the country which released the first nuclear missile, Lil slips the note back across the table. At first, I think that we've managed to go undetected, I really do, but at that moment, Professor Cattaro snaps out of his droning voice and loudly says, 'STOP!'

A couple of low-ranked students jump – Sam included – and look around to see what could have possibly made the professor halt in the middle of his lecture. I see a few monitors pulse a brighter blue as the students react with weak surprise. But I know, of course, why Professor Cattaro has interrupted the lesson. My hand is still on top of the note and I wonder if I can somehow slip it into my pocket without him noticing. But the professor is already beside my desk, holding out his hand. Fighting the hint of embarrassment which seeks to trickle into my body, I pass him the note and he looks down his long nose at me. His greying hair falls forward and into his eyes.

'Note passing, Eve? How incredibly junior school of you.'

I stare straight ahead and am pleased to note that my monitor remains a cool shade of blue. Perhaps I am regaining some of the control I had lost. Perhaps there is hope for me in the wake of the harvest after all.

'Sorry, Professor.'

'What is so important that you need to share it in the middle of a revision lecture? Need I remind you that the harvest is coming up at the end of this cycle?'

'No, sir,' I say quietly. 'Sorry.'

I assume that he is going to throw the note in the bin, but instead the professor starts unfolding the paper and I realise belatedly that he is going to read it. I glance over at Lil but she seems unperturbed by the whole scenario. I resist the compulsion to crawl under my desk.

'Let's see. *Do you think he could be a mask?* Very interesting question, Eve. Perhaps you were asking a legitimate question about the class after all? Hmm? If the North Korean dictator was a *mask*, perhaps?' Professor Cattaro's tone of voice suggests that he certainly does not think that the question relates to the politics of the *old world*.

'Well, let's see if Lilu got it right, shall we?'

For founders' sake, he is going to read the note aloud. I watch Lil out of the corner of my eye – she dislikes being called by her full name – but her face remains impassive. I turn my attention back to Professor Cattaro, for despite the humility of the situation, I *am* curious to find out what her answer is.

'*He's just a ladder-climber, you are being paranoid. Forget about him.*'

I sag down in my seat. So Lil doesn't think that there's anything to be worried about after all. Her silence at the breakfast table this morning wasn't an indication of her concern, but something else. Disinterest, probably.

'Well there we have it, everyone, the North Korean dictator according to Lilu was a ladder climber.' The class is silent and the professor throws the note into the recycling bin. 'I suggest you all think very carefully about who you choose as your study partners; the harvest is serious business. Lilu and Eve – as a consequence, you will both lose your leisure time for the next two weeks. You can use the additional volunteer hours to reflect upon the type of life you will be destined for next year if you underperform in the harvest.'

Two weeks for passing a note? That's harsh, even by Professor Cattaro's standards. And was it worth it?

He's just a ladder-climber. That's what Lil had written. *Forget about him.* He must be, of course, because the other possibilities are too awful.

But as I write down the factors that led to the Third War, I can't help glancing back at the page with the three columns. Ladder Climber. Informer. *Mask.*

My flexi-screen beeps and I look across to see a new alert.

Infraction recorded.
Consequence: Double duties.
Period: Two weeks

I sigh and send the alert skittering across the screen. At least I'm rostered on at the preschool this evening.

I focus all of my attention on Professor Cattaro's droning

voice for the rest of the class. Well, almost all of it. Sometimes, between taking notes, I stare at the back of Sam's head, wondering what he is thinking. When the professor had read out the note, he hadn't reacted in any visible way. Perhaps he didn't know that we were talking about him after all. Perhaps he really is on the leaderboard and I just missed his name.

When the bell finally rings and the class trickles outside, Lil is annoyed. Of course, there is nothing on her face to show this, and her monitor remains a calm blue, but I have known her too well for far too long not to recognise that the toss of dark hair over her shoulder and her short, quick steps are symptoms of her carefully suppressed anger.

'Stay away from me,' she says under her breath as she walks past me and out into the courtyard.

She does have a partial reason for being annoyed; the infraction has already pushed her down to number three on the leaderboard, and I am teetering at the edge of the elite. However, I refuse to take all of the blame – Lil could have thrown the note out rather than responding.

My gaze falls on Sam, who is now lining up at the nutrition line, waiting for his lunch.

I step into place behind him, wondering if I have the guts to ask him the question that is burning within me. I glance at the leaderboard situated behind the servers, see my name in the sixth position, and decide that I need to settle this once and for all before my curiosity pushes me down even further.

'So,' I say carefully, and Sam turns, his brow creasing slightly, 'what's it like working for the overseers?'

He is silent, and I wonder if he is going to deny it or simply ignore me. And then he does something I'm not expecting. He laughs. It's an odd sound, and I glance down at his monitor to see if it's a true laugh or if he is just doing it to throw me off. The sleeve of his jumpsuit covers any tell-tale signs of infractions.

'Why do you think I'm working for the overseers?' The line moves forward and Sam scans his ID card, collecting his mid-day tray of food and vitamins.

'Are you telling me that you aren't?' I'm not about to disclose my thoughts on why he might be watching me, about why the overseers might want a little more information than what they can procure simply from my monitor report.

'Of course not.'

I don't believe him. After my redline during the harvest, the overseers will be wanting to keep an eye on me. Or perhaps Sia was unconvinced by my claim that I couldn't feel anything, maybe there was some sort of sign that showed her that I was feeling empty and heavy at the same time. The overseers have probably cut him some sort of deal; report back on Eve and we will boost your ranking. Should I ask him if he's a *mask*? I decide to take a different tack. Stick with the facts, Eve.

'I know that you aren't on the leaderboard.' I collect my tray too, and we move across the courtyard together.

'What do you mean? Of course I'm on the leaderboard. Everyone's on the leaderboard.' His voice is light and I am almost convinced.

'I checked,' I say evenly. 'Twice.'

He looks at me, his eyes more blue than grey today. I was right, they must change in the light. 'So you spent, what – half an hour? An hour? – scanning through the leaderboard, looking for my name. I'm flattered, Eve, but I thought curiosity wasn't a desired virtue in Eridu.' He places his tray on a table and gestures towards the group of elite, sitting at their usual table. They don't appear to be paying any attention to us, but I know that they will be watching, wondering why I'm speaking to a ladder climber. Lil isn't there, she must have gone off to spend her lunchtime elsewhere so that she didn't have to sit with me. Doubt fills my mind; perhaps I didn't check the names carefully enough. This whole thing is just ridiculous.

'You'd better join the elite.'

The way he says it is almost a sneer. 'Stay away from me,' I say, coldly, echoing Lil's words.

But I'm not sure if he heard me, because he already has the Book of Eridu open, and seems engrossed by the words on the page.

I saw humans blow up other humans. I will never, ever, be able to get that image out of my mind.

Book of Eridu

XV

I have little time to think about Sam and his ranking – or lack of one, as the case may be – over the next few days. The double duties keep me busy, and although I can't shake the feeling that he's watching me at the institute, thankfully I'm not rostered on with him after school again. Each time that I'm tempted to search the leaderboard for his name again, I tell myself firmly that it doesn't matter; that it is of no concern to me. I spend each day focusing on staying blue, and eventually I manage to claw my way back up into third position on the leaderboard. It's not amazing, but it's acceptable enough this early in the cycle. Tara, who was in sixth place, drops down to seventh and a new student named Ty joins the elite.

Aside from my extra duties, I am also preoccupied with helping to prepare for the dedication ceremony. With the previous cycle being harvested, there is now room for the pre-schoolers to move up to the institute. A new round of births is scheduled as well, so it is necessary for everyone to be moving forward in their cycle.

It's like the hands of the clocks in the *old world* moving continuously around in repetitive loops, and I become more aware than usual of the way that we are governed by cycles. There are the cycles I've always thought about, the cycles at the institute. But life is also one big cycle, ticking closer to transfer. The thought sends a little chill down my spine.

During the ceremony itself, I volunteer to help the teachers

93

organise the children backstage. Tali is there, as are all the other five-year-olds, the less restrained ones giggling and bouncing around in excitement. 'Shhhh,' I say, and Tali squeals and runs over to me.

I allow her to throw her arms around me, for the final time. Once she receives her monitor, she will be under the close scrutiny of her professors, architects, and perhaps even the overseers. I don't need to be another person in her life telling her not to feel; at least, not today.

I watch from the side of the stage as the newly harvested overseer, Ida, co-runs the ceremony under the watchful eyes of the older overseers. I recognise her as one of the elite from the last cycle. I wonder how she feels about Luc being culled.

'The founders knew how important it was to control our emotions,' she begins, and the gathering in the auditorium becomes silent. 'We know from their notes that Alexa was the first founder to recognise the need to suppress the stronger feelings that for so many years had been accepted as part of human nature. Of course, we all know where those strong emotions led our ancestors.'

I can't see the audience, from here, but I can imagine my guardians nodding in agreement.

'Thank Alexa,' says Ida.

'Thank Alexa,' we repeat, dutifully.

'We soon learnt that emotions were a form of sickness which needed to be cured if we wished to create a better society than the one our ancestors had destroyed. Now, from the outside, it can be difficult to judge when someone is experiencing sicknesses such as sadness, grief, excitement, or love. There are the tell-tale symptoms, of course, but mere observation alone does not provide concrete evidence of these emotions having been experienced.'

I nod, thinking of my guardians. They are so skilled at keeping their faces blank that I would be none the wiser if they were experiencing some sort of strong emotion. I can only hope that one day, I too will be as disciplined as them.

'And so,' continues Ida, 'many years after the founders had passed on, our scientists designed something revolutionary. As you know, everyone in their first year at the institute receives a monitor implanted in their left wrist.' Ida holds up her arm to demonstrate, and then looks at it quizzically, as though surprised to find that her arm is bare. I suppose after so many years of wearing the monitor, it must feel strange to have it removed.

'Today, our five-year-olds will be going through the dedication ceremony,' she says, dropping her arm back to her side. 'They will dedicate themselves to the six virtues in front of their guardians, future professors, overseers, and peers. Afterwards, our medics will surgically implant their monitors; this is the first important step in their journey to harvest.'

I feel something touch my hand and I look down to see that Tali has crept out of line in order to slip her chubby hand into my own. Her eyes are wide, so I crouch down and quickly whisper in her ear.

'It doesn't hurt, not really. It's hardly surgery, just a slight slit in the skin so that the sensor can pick up all the signals it needs.'

I show her my wrist, indicating how the top part of the bracelet can move slightly forward and back, while the underneath is fixed.

'The sensor has thin wires,' I explain in a hushed whisper, 'smaller than a strand of hair. They reach out beneath your skin and receive data from inside.'

Tali still looks pale, and a single tear hovers on her lower eyelid. Oh for founders' sake, she's about to go on stage so I need to keep her calm. 'To be honest, the injection you are given to numb the area hurts more than the monitor itself, and you've had injections before, haven't you?'

She nods.

'Quick, now, pop back into line.'

Tali rubs her hand across her face and the tear disappears, then she throws her arms around me again. I don't bother pushing her away, but I do wonder if her guardians show her too much leniency. I've never met a child who tries to hug me so much; she'll have to grow out of it pretty quickly at the institute if she wants to do well.

One of the preschool teachers sends the first child in the line out onto the stage and the rest obediently follow. I carefully guide Tali back into her place, and she drops into step behind one of her friends. I form a small knot with the preschool teachers and we watch, huddled behind the curtain. I just hope that all the children behave.

'Welcome,' says Ida, 'and founders' speed.'

'Founders' speed,' repeat the children automatically, in a singsong way. They line up across the centre of the stage.

'Today, in front of your teachers, guardians, and the rest of the community, you are all going to dedicate yourself to the six virtues. As daughters and sons of the founders, it is your responsibility to uphold their values and be the best versions of yourselves that you can be.'

The children look up at her, wide-eyed. One girl fidgets with her jumpsuit, and then stands still.

'First, the virtue of restraint.'

I can see the symbol for the six virtues projected on the screen at the back of the stage, the converging triangles more significant than ever.

'Practising restraint is important because sometimes it is tempting to say something that you shouldn't, or, more likely, to *feel* something dangerous. We all need to control our urges so that we can lead the future of humanity in peace. Do you dedicate yourselves to the virtue of restraint?'

'We do,' say the little voices.

'The second virtue is productivity. Idleness is an easy trap to fall into, but those who are lazy and do not do their fair share are not the sort of people that we desire in Eridu. As you are well aware, humanity with purpose is one of our key mantras. Do you dedicate yourselves to the virtue of productivity?'

'We do,' echo the children.

And so she continues through the six virtues and I find my mind lurching back into the past, to the ceremony when I first received my monitor. I hardly remember anything about the ceremony itself, but I do recall the fierceness with which I pledged myself to those virtues; purity, patience, productivity, sacrifice, restraint and contentment – the building blocks of a peaceful society. As a child, I had watched my brother carefully and was ready to follow in his footsteps, to be an outstanding citizen and always remain blue.

'The trick,' Luc had told me on the morning of the ceremony, 'is to remove yourself from the situation. Whenever you feel the beginnings of a strong emotion, view it as a dream, or as though it is happening to somebody else.' And so I had, and it had worked out perfectly. Many students are apprehensive of being ranked, but I had known with complete certainty that as soon as my name hit that leaderboard it would be right at the top.

Of course, it didn't work out so perfectly for Luc after all.

'Do you dedicate yourselves to the virtue of contentment?' asks Ida.

'We do,' say the children, and I whisper the words under my breath as well. In this cycle, more than any of the previous cycles, it is important that I uphold the virtues.

'These children of the founders have dedicated themselves to the six virtues in front of their community. This afternoon they will receive their monitors, and tomorrow they will begin their tutoring under the watchful eyes of the professors at the institute. Praise Alexa.'

'Praise Alexa.'

The children file off stage and Tali beams at me. 'I did it, Eve.'

'Well done, kiddo.'

I realise that I'm going to miss seeing her at the preschool.

Her guardians file through the side door a moment later, and I excuse myself. They can have the job of keeping Tali calm while the medics implant the monitor; I have my own duties to prepare for.

The Third War. The darkness. The virus. Maybe humanity is supposed to die out now; perhaps we have reached our limit. But I'm not going down without a fight.

Book of Eridu

XVI

On the night of the dedication ceremony, Sam is rostered on with me for dinner duties. It unnerves me a little, but I give myself a firm shake; as long as I keep my monitor blue and my mouth shut, then there is nothing to be concerned about – even if he is an informer.

'Hello, Eve,' he says when I arrive at my duty, and I note that the last words we exchanged don't seem to have changed his demeanour at all.

'Hi, Sam, haven't seen you around much lately, outside the institute.'

He shrugs. 'I've been working at the vertical farms, mostly, picking vegetables and so on.' He gestures towards the carrots in the warming dish in front of us. 'Who knows, maybe I was partially responsible for growing those.' He smiles at me too easily, and I look away.

'That sounds like the perfect position for someone who doesn't have a ranking.'

He doesn't deny it, and I don't look at him, but I can hear the smile in his voice as he says, 'Oh yes, much like working dinner duties.'

He's right, serving up the allocated meals isn't exactly a difficult duty, fit for the skills of the highly-ranked, but we all invariably end up working in a range of different occupations around Eridu while studying at the institute. We work together in silence, and I wonder if I was too hasty in accusing him of informing for the overseers.

We are still serving the last few people when a loud alarm ricochets off the walls and I jump slightly. I control my breathing, and then glance down at my monitor. I can only hope that it stayed blue. The sound is piercing, and I resist the urge to cover my ears; the overseers – or at least any potential informers – will be watching. I glance to my left; yes, Sam is definitely watching me. Maybe I wasn't so hasty after all. I reach one hand into my pocket and retrieve the Lortnok. Squishing it slightly between my fingers to crack the case, I place it in my mouth. The bitter liquid floods onto my tongue and I nearly gag.

Swallowing quickly, I take a deep breath and, as I've been taught, step out of my body, observing the room from afar.

The group of harvested adults hasn't moved and neither have the children playing chasey around the tables. Of course they haven't, the adults all had their stims removed after the harvest, and the children are too young to have even received the temporary stims they will be assigned soon after they arrive at the institute. It's clear in my mind; this is just another test.

The unranked students are mostly frozen in place, looking glassy-eyed into the distance as they fight to keep their emotions in check. They aren't old enough to appear on a leaderboard yet, but it is only through practice that they can prepare. There are a couple of amber alerts here and there, but no redliners; not yet, anyway.

'Why did you do that?' asks Sam.

'Shhh.'

I glance over at the tight knot of grey in the centre of the room. The elite are eating dinner and chatting easily, pretending that there is nothing at all to be concerned about. The alarm continues to screech, as though some dire emergency is taking place. I become vaguely aware of Sam saying something else to me, but I ignore him for now; perhaps he can succeed in the tests with little effort, but the control doesn't come to me so easily these days, and I need to do everything within my power to make sure I don't go amber again.

Then Sam places a hand on my arm and I fall back into my body. He peers into my face and I notice that the blue in his eyes is so pale that it is almost translucent. I haven't seen anybody with that colour eyes before.

'Eve, are you okay?'

'Don't touch me. I need to concentrate.'

He frowns, and then I realise that if he is working with the overseers, that this is the perfect opportunity to regain a few points – surely carrying out a conversation with him while remaining blue would push me up the ranks higher than just staring into the distance. I am determined to do well, so I take a deep breath. 'Sorry, what were you saying?'

'You took something.'

'*Self-destruct sequence set for two minutes.*' The voice is robotic and booming. I try to keep track of my conversation with Sam, but it is difficult when my attention is distracted by the piercing crescendo of the siren.

'Don't worry, it was prescribed by the medics. You can check.'

I am well aware of instances where students have been prescribed particular vitamins only to palm them off to others in payment for mentoring; a black market of vitamins that is firmly frowned upon.

'But why?' he asks, as though he genuinely cares.

The ceiling above me creaks loudly, but I try to keep my focus on Sam. There is a rumble and then a cascade of explosions, as though bombs are going off in each corner of the room. The roof groans again, and I close my eyes as I feel the rush of air that tells me that the ceiling is starting to collapse in on me.

'Not that I really need to tell you,' I say, opening my eyes and holding his gaze, 'but it's to help with my emotional control.' I keep my voice light.

'So you are starting to feel something?'

I don't like his tone of voice – it almost sounds hopeful.

I see the steel beam directly above me warp and fall. I look down at the floor and refuse to flinch.

'Are you sure you're okay?'

The room goes silent and the students exhale a collective sigh of relief. Focusing my full attention back on Sam, I lift the edges of my mouth and nod.

'Of course I'm okay. See?' I pull the sleeve of my jumpsuit up to demonstrate that my monitor has remained blessedly blue throughout the test. He almost looks disappointed. 'And what about you?' I ask. For someone who isn't on the leaderboard, he seems peculiarly invested in my emotional control and ranking.

He doesn't respond to my question. 'Do you want to sit with me over dinner?' he asks instead.

The question takes me by surprise, and I look at him, eyebrow raised; then I look over at the elite, where my rightful chair is. He sees my glance. 'That's okay, you go sit with your friends.'

If he's low-ranked, then it's a ridiculous suggestion anyway. But I am torn, because if he's working for the overseers, then it's probably not the best idea to refuse him. Either way, though, he must know that it's expected for the highly ranked students to sit together.

'Sam, why aren't you on the leaderboard?' I try again.

He shrugs. Then he pulls up the sleeve of his jumpsuit and

shows me the bare skin that lies beneath. I don't even know where
to begin. My skin goes cold, and I step away from him.

'Go sit with your friends. Really, it was foolish of me to ask.'

There's an odd tone in his voice, but I can't quite place it.

'Yes, it was.'

And I turn away from the informer and join the elite.

XVII

It's settled then; the reason that Sam isn't on the leaderboard has nothing to do with his monitor being broken, it's that he doesn't have a monitor at all. He's definitely not a ladder-climber. I think back to his reactions during the test at dinner time. Perhaps he doesn't have a stim, either.

Informer? Mask? I mull these over in my thoughts, prodding the revelation this way and that, trying to work out a satisfactory explanation. It's clear in my mind that he is watching me. My guardians might know something, but if I asked them I know what they would say. *Curiosity isn't a virtue, Eve. Be content.*

When I receive my breakfast allocation the next morning, there is something missing.

'Hana, did you forget something?'

Hana smiles at me. 'Oh, sorry, Eve.'

She takes the tray back, glancing over the instructions on the screen, and then shakes her head.

'No, nothing is missing.'

She really can be incompetent sometimes. I can't believe that I used to associate with her. But of course, that was before it all mattered.

'I put in a request this morning for another vitamin.' I lower my voice, although I'm not really sure why. 'For the Lortnok.'

Her face brightens. 'Oh yes, I can see here that you have put the request through for a double dose.'

I relax.

Hana leans slightly forward, over the counter, her big green eyes full of some emotion. Compassion? 'But, Eve, your request has been denied.'

Denied. Great. I am tempted to ask her to check again, and to keep checking until the screen displays what I want – need – it to show. Instead, I calmly take the tray and walk over to the elite, trying to ignore the way my heart is hammering uncomfortably in my chest cavity. It'll be okay, it was only a temporary fix anyway. I haven't gone amber since that morning at the transfer centre. *But that was before the Lortnok,* says a little voice in my mind. I briefly entertain the thought of asking the other elite if any of them take Lortnok and can give me one of theirs, just for today. It's frowned upon, of course, but what's worse? Struggling with my emotions for the day or being in trouble with the overseers.

I place my tray of food on the table and slip in beside Lil. Blank face, Eve. Feel nothing. I can't help but think that the sudden cancelled prescription might have something to do with Sam.

'Eve!'

I turn around in my seat and see Tali running over to me, golden ringlets quivering as usual.

'Tali, how are you?' I ask, glad for the distraction from my thoughts. 'Prepared for your first day at the institute?'

She rocks forward on her toes, as though too excited to stand flat on the ground. Then she notices the glances of the other students that I'm sitting with, and she looks guiltily at the amber monitor on her wrist. Screwing her eyes tightly shut, she breathes deeply, and a moment later her monitor is blue again. Very good, little one.

'How are you feeling?' I ask.

'Great,' she says with enthusiasm, then she checks herself, rearranging her face into a neutral expression. 'I mean, fine thank you.'

The elite nod at her encouragingly, but there's a sinking feeling in my stomach.

'Anyway, I just wanted to say hi.'

And with that, she turns and walks back to a table where her guardians are sitting, ringlets bobbing frantically in her wake.

I have a bit of trouble concentrating throughout the day. The heaviness returns, worse than before, and I try to make a medic appointment to have my Lortnok prescription re-instated, but there are no availabilities until the next day.

To make matters worse, I'm rostered on at the transfer centre again. I can only hope that there are no clients scheduled for a transfer and that I'm simply updating the system files again.

Sam is already at the centre when I arrive. It doesn't feel like a coincidence. According to the schedule, I will only be training him for the first hour, and then I will be on my own in the second. Got to love the double duties. I scan my ID card.

'Hi, Eve,' says a female voice. My stomach sinks, but I already know who the voice belongs to before I turn around. It's Octavia, which can only mean one thing.

'We are blessed with a transfer this afternoon.'

Blessed. 'Praise Alexa.'

I smile hollowly and work on calming my breathing. *In for six. Hold for six. Out for six. Repeat.* If I can control my breathing, I can control my emotions. *In for six. Hold for six. Out for six.*

'Your trainee is waiting for you in the back room,' explains Octavia. 'If you don't mind briefing him, I have the transfer in the chamber already, and his past dependant and partner are set to arrive soon.'

'No problem,' I reply, feeling pleased with the way I am handling myself so far. Octavia, dressed in blue, nods at me before disappearing through the sliding doors.

I enter the room where we updated the codes just a few days before. Sam is sitting easily at one of the desks.

'Hello again, Sam,' I say, and my voice comes out colder than I planned. Oh well, he deserves it for lying to me about being on the leaderboard.

Sam looks at me quizzically for a moment. 'Hello, Eve.' His voice is quiet and I wonder vaguely at his change of disposition

'So I'm guessing that you'll tell me that you've never seen a transfer before?'

He seems to weigh up his response, before replying. 'No, but I've read all about it. I understand the process.'

He is an informer for the overseers and I know that I can't believe anything that he says.

'Well,' I explain dutifully, because he'll be reporting back on how well I'm doing my job. 'Our main job is to brief the family on the process and provide reassurance where required. Octavia will deal with the transfer, and we will look after the dependant and his partner.'

Sam nods. Rising slowly, he crosses the room to stand in front of me. He doesn't say anything, just stares at me in an unnerving way, so I continue explaining the procedure.

'Then there will be a short ceremony – you will probably be gone by then as you are only here for an hour. The transfer will take place, we test the file, and the family leaves. Then Mr -' I check the name on my display, 'Mr Wang will perform his final productive duty for society, and there are a few forms to fill out. And that's about it.'

Sam is still watching me closely and I feel the stirrings of some emotion bubbling beneath the surface. I sort through the symptoms in my mind. Irritation. Annoyance. Something like that. I take a breath and will my body to relax.

'It bothers you,' says Sam.

'We have already been through this. I'm fine.'

He glances at the monitor on my wrist. 'Your heart rate is elevated. Your breathing is shallower, more rapid than usual. Pupils are dilated, too. Just admit it. Or do you want to risk being harvested as a transfer agent?'

I mentally berate my disobedient pupils, pulling my sleeve down over my monitor. It is still glowing blue, but he is correct, it has started to pulse at a slightly faster rate and the hue has become more intense than usual.

In for six, hold for six, out for six. If only I had the Lortnok. First I'm denied the memrase procedure, and now the only thing that has helped me cope over the past few days too. Do the overseers want me to drop down the leaderboard? Do they want me to be culled at the end of the cycle? Perhaps I should ask Sam, maybe he would know.

A dull clanging sound echoes around the building, indicating the arrival of the family in the foyer and interrupting my thoughts. I turn abruptly, thankful for a reason to escape the metallic scrutiny in Sam's stare.

'After you,' I say.

Before following Sam out into the corridor I take a moment to compose myself. I close my eyes, breathe deeply, and carefully reconstruct a few of the slowly crumbling walls within my mind. It'll be fine; it's just a routine transfer. There is nothing to be concerned about at all.

Even without the Lortnok, Mr Wang's dependant, Ben, turns out to be an easy client. He is confident in the transfer process and needs little in terms of either information or consolation. Still, he *is* thankful for the ceremonial drink and listens attentively to the spiel I am required to read out. Mr Wang's partner doesn't show, and I wonder if she has already gone through the memrase procedure.

'Today is a day of celebration,' I begin dutifully, speaking clearly because I am well aware that my speech is being recorded for anyone to be able to access on their flexi-screens. It will be stored alongside his transfer file so that it's available for anybody who might like to view it in the future. 'Mr Wang has reached the sixth and final stage of life.' The words of the final transition appear on my screen, with information about the client already entered where appropriate. I speak about his job as a biologist, his success as a guardian, and his calm disposition.

'His life has been productive and fruitful,' I conclude, 'and he will forever be remembered as a valued citizen of Eridu. In all ways, Mr Wang has upheld Eridu's aspiration, humanity with purpose.'

I direct the dependant over to the window where he can watch the transfer take place. His guardian is lying on a bed with metallic wires sprouting out of his temples. When Mr Wang sees us at the window, he raises one hand in a gesture of either greeting or farewell. I glance at his dependant, Ben, standing next to me, but he is calm and accepting. He has faith in the system. They always do.

Octavia flicks the switch and Mr Wang is transferred. Ben gazes through the window at his guardian's now lifeless body with no emotion. Of course, we all know that the shell isn't really him, that his essence has been automatically sent to the Grid the moment Octavia pressed the button. I ignore the prickles of goosebumps erupting on my arms. Sending the consciousness to the Grid is the easy part; the tricky bit is creating the transfer file which will allow anyone in Eridu to speak with him long after the body has disintegrated. I stare closely at the shell, but it is perfectly still now that the essence has been emptied out of him. I relax; nothing out of the ordinary is going to occur. Not today.

I escort the dependant into the waiting room while Octavia tests the file and a few minutes later another client leaves the centre, content that his guardian's consciousness is stored forever in the Grid, accessible through the transfer program in his flexi-screen.

Sam stays the entire time, watching the process with open curiosity; it must be nice not to have a monitor. Of course, even if it really is Sam's first transfer, it doesn't mean much. It's quite possible to have never seen a transfer before if your grand-guardian had transferred before you were born, and you were low-ranked or the overseers had decided you were more suitable for other duties.

When it is over, we walk outside and begin heading towards Block A in silence.

'So, was it what you expected?' I ask him eventually, as the pools of light from the roof of the tunnel flicker over his face.

'Yes, and no,' he replies. 'Things always look different outside the pages of a book. It really is a marvel, though.'

'Sure is,' I say, keeping my tone even. 'Praise the founders.'

He is silent and I suppress the urge to roll my eyes.

'So why don't you like it?' he asks again.

I am sick of the continued pressure to respond to his questions. Not only is it impolite, but I have zero interest in reliving the experience that has resulted in my dislike of the centre.

'Curiosity killed the cat,' I say, trying to keep things light-hearted.

'Cats went extinct a long time ago.'

I sigh, but I think back to what he said earlier. He's right; the last thing I want is to be harvested as a transfer agent, and if he's working for the overseers then this is the perfect opportunity to let him know this. I decide to take the plunge, hoping that I won't regret it.

'My first transfer was…' I search for the word… Traumatic? Too strong. Sickening? 'Complicated,' I say at last.

A pool of light illuminates Sam's face and I can see his raised eyebrow. He's good at that.

'He didn't want to be transferred,' I explained. 'But of course, the oxygen credits…'

Now we are walking through a dark portion of the tunnel, so I can't see his face, but I assume that he is nodding.

Of course, we all become highly aware of the importance of oxy-creds from a young age. 'They're kind of like money, aren't they,' muses Sam.

'No,' I say, my voice louder than I intended. I'm a little shocked that he could make such a comparison after all the damage caused by money. But then again, if he's a bit slow… 'Money was the catalyst for inequality,' I continue. 'Oxy-creds are to ensure productivity. Anyway, the transfer's level of productivity was no longer offsetting the resources required to sustain him.'

'You sound like a textbook.'

Of course I do. 'His past dependant was nearing forty. She wanted to apply for her own partner and dependants. But her job didn't allow them enough credits to bring a child into the world without some… sacrifices.'

'But that's fairly normal isn't it?' replies Sam. 'I read about it in the Book. Even having some uncertainty over the procedure is common. That's why you have the ceremony. What went wrong?'

I weigh up how much I'll be able to tell him before I risk going amber. I want him to realise how incompatible I am with this duty, in case he really does have some say in my future.

'Well, the client was upset, and even the ceremony did little to calm him down,' I explain as we walk through the tunnel. 'Even with sedation, Octavia had to strap him to the bed to keep him still while she performed the transfer.'

'I see,' says Sam. 'That would be shocking for your first transfer.'

Should I just leave it at that? Is that enough to ensure that I won't ever be harvested as a transfer agent? I decide to keep going. 'Octavia got me to test the file, and the family left, content with the service.'

'Okay,' said Sam. 'And then?'

'I was filling out the forms on my flexi-screen,' I explain. 'But there was one bit of information that I was confused about so I went back into the chamber to ask for Octavia's help.'

I take a deep breath, steadying my voice, making sure that my monitor remains blue. So far, so good.

'The client was on a trolley, naked, and Octavia was preparing to wheel him through to perform the final duty.'

'You mean the shell was on a trolley,' Sam says quietly, and I curse myself.

'Yes, his shell. The only problem was, when I started walking into the room the shell sat up. Started screaming worse than before the transfer. I was in so much shock that I just stood there half in the doorway while Octavia did something I couldn't see and then the screaming stopped.'

Sam is silent.

'I finished the forms by myself.'

'Have you told anyone about this?' His voice is even and gives me no clue as to what he is thinking.

'Only my guardians,' I respond evenly.

'And what did they say?'

I shrug nonchalantly, meeting Sam's eyes with my own. 'They explained that sometimes the nerves and muscles in the shell continue to flex for a few minutes after the transfer. He wasn't really there, of course, it was just a biological reaction.'

Sam is watching me closely, as if evaluating my response.

'My prime told me that sometimes the shells struggle to let go… The thing is, I was only thirteen when I was first rostered on to work at the transfer centre,' I explain. 'I know now that there is nothing to be concerned about, and I have complete faith in the transfer process. However,' I make sure that my voice is calm and sincere as I say this, 'I would really appreciate it if you would pass onto the overseers that I have no interest in being harvested as a transfer agent.'

'I'll do whatever I can,' he says. Is that confirmation that he is an informer? 'So,' says Sam, 'have you talked to Luc yet?'

I stop in the centre of the path, my feet adhered to the concrete surface like the roots of a tree. I am content. I am content.

'I don't know what you're talking about.'

'Sure you do. You remember. I know that you remember so there is no point in denying it.'

I simultaneously want to run into Block A, and crawl into the base of the tunnel, and inflict pain on the person standing next to me. I stare hard at the tunnel wall, and my monitor remains blue. The tunnel stretches out before me, seemingly endless and I feel incredibly tired.

Sam walks around until he is standing in front of me. I stare straight through him.

'Eve,' he says gently, and I imagine a man in a gas mask walking up behind him, gun aimed point-blank at the back of his head. 'I never had a brother. From what I know about Eridu, most people don't. You are lucky to have had that bond with someone.'

The man pulls the trigger and Sam falls to the ground, twitching slightly as the blood creeps outwards, staining the floor of the tunnel.

'Eve, are you listening to me?'

I step around him and walk quickly towards Block A.

XVIII

When I enter the apartment, my eyes centre on that vacant space below my pod. I've actively avoided looking at it since the harvest, my eyes sliding diligently from the door on one side to my desk on the other, without truly seeing the emptiness between. This afternoon, I am drawn to it like the moths in the Insectarium hover around the lights in the roof of the enclosure. Something is different.

And then I see it, on the wall behind where Luc's pod used to be. Since the pod was removed, there has just been a cool, grey substrate. But not anymore. I get closer and notice the little dark plants that have started to take hold in the space where Luc's pod used to be. Just a couple of weeks ago I was able to see the steel of the bracket that held up Luc's pod, but now the plants have completely taken over. My guardians will be pleased; the more plants, the more oxy-credits.

My heart thunders uncomfortably in my chest, and before I know what I am doing, I am ripping the plants out of the wall and tossing them onto the ground, revealing the steel bracket beneath. I don't stop until the entire metal structure is clear of the foliage. And then I feel an intense urge to throw up.

I make it to the bathroom just in time, and the sandwiches that I ate for lunch make a quick reappearance. Although my stomach is soon empty, I continue to retch and gag for another few minutes until hot tears are squeezed out of the corners of my eyes. Eventually, I lie still on the cool concrete floor in exhaustion. What is wrong with me? Something must have been off in the food that I ate earlier. Or perhaps I should book myself in for an appointment with the medic.

Thank the founders that my guardians aren't home from work yet, I don't know what they would say if they found me lying on the bathroom floor smelling like vomit. They would certainly have to tell the overseers. I glance at the monitor on my wrist; it is glowing blue, but I realise the exertion of throwing up would have elevated my heart rate and may have set off the sensors. I will likely have some explaining to do.

I clean myself up and return to the main room, working out in my mind which part of the homework I'm going to do first. But once again, as soon as I see the small dark plants now lying on the floor in the empty space below my pod, my body reacts violently. This time, rather than throwing up, it feels like something is squeezing all the air out of my lungs so that I can't breathe. I sit down hard on the floor and put my head between my knees, trying to suck in deep breaths while feeling like I'm falling, falling down into nothingness.

'Restraint of- restraint of-' I'm so desperate to draw breath into my lungs that I can't even get the familiar words out of my mouth. The lights on my monitor are glowing red now, and I try desperately to detach myself from the situation, to see myself as an objective observer. But the technique that has usually worked for me is failing me today. There are prickles of electricity cascading down my arms like the rains from the *old world*.

What's that sound? Is it a knock on the door? Oh for founder's sake, it's probably my guardians.

'Eve, are you alright?'

The voice is unfamiliar and I realise belatedly that my guardians wouldn't knock on their own apartment door. I'm really not with it today; it must be the food poisoning.

I try to call out, to say that I'm fine and just to leave me alone. Okay, that I'm not quite fine, but I will be in just a moment as soon as I have myself under control. But I can't seem to draw enough air into my lungs to get the words out. I lift my head and notice a red patch on the leg of my jumpsuit. Raising one hand to my face, I discover that blood is streaming out of my nose. Not again. And then I know with complete certainty that I'm dying. Nobody has ever died in Eridu but I know that it is true and some sort of feeling rockets through my body. The red on my monitor is so bright I can hardly notice it pulsing at all.

The door opens and a woman in blue enters the room. At least it's not an overseer. Her face remains impassive but I think I see a slight dilation of the pupils which indicates that she is as surprised as I am to find out that someone is dying in Eridu.

It's Sia, I realise belatedly, the medic who was going to perform the memrase procedure. I feel a rush of some sort of emotion, and don't even attempt to stifle it. If they had allowed me to have the procedure, then I wouldn't be sitting on the floor of my unit dying right now. It's all their fault, whoever the person in red was who interrupted my procedure.

Sia drops to one knee and opens a small dark case that I didn't notice her holding. I feel another surge of something. What is the emotion called? Hope, perhaps. Of course a medic will be able to stop me from dying, that's her job.

My hands are shaking as the woman fills a syringe with a clear liquid and taps the side of it.

'Please don't… let… me…. die…' I finally get out, between half-drawn breaths.

Sia doesn't answer me, instead unbuttoning my jumpsuit so that she can access my upper arm. I hardly feel the sting of the needle before descending into blessed darkness where I will no longer be able to feel. My last thought before my consciousness winks out is that perhaps this is what it feels like to be floating in the amniotic tanks.

XIX

When I wake up, I have no idea where I am.

I'm not lying on the hard, concrete floor of my apartment. It's dark, but it doesn't feel like I'm cocooned in my own private pod either. There is a beeping sound coming from somewhere to my right, but I can't see anything at all. I try to move, but I seem to be paralysed. Am I dead after all?

'No, Eve, you aren't dead.'

I jump; I must have spoken aloud. I feel cool hands on my face and a moment later I can see again. The room is small and sterile and the beeping sound is coming from a machine beside my bed that is covered in colourful lights. I try to sit up, but realise the reason I can't move is because there are straps holding me down.

'They were for your own safety,' Sia explains. 'We weren't sure how you would react when you woke up.'

There are many things I would like to say in response, but I swallow them all before I get myself into even more trouble than I'm already in. Sia's gaze rests on the machine next to me, and whatever she sees there must be adequate because a moment later she begins to loosen the bonds. I take a deep breath as the straps are removed and sit up, propping a pillow behind my back. It smells like antiseptic and cleaning products. I hate hospitals.

And then I notice all of the additional… equipment… attached to me. As well as the usual monitor on my wrist, there is a larger device of some kind strapped firmly to my arm, an array

119

of wires sprouting from my temples and a cannula sticking out of my hand.

'This seems… intense.' My voice comes out in a raw croak.

The medic doesn't answer me, instead retrieving a flexi-screen from the bedside table, unfolding it and scrolling through quickly. She hasn't enabled the concealment function so I can see an assortment of lines and dots through the back of the transparent screen. It doesn't matter, anyway, I can't make out what any of it means.

I clear my throat. 'Do you think I will be back at Block A in time for dinner?'

Sia averts her attention from the screen for a moment. 'I'm afraid you missed dinner,' she says lightly. 'You've been under observation for the past twenty hours since the incident.'

The incident? Ah yes, the incident where I went *old world* crazy. Again. I have enough presence of mind not to feel ashamed. With all the monitors on me, the slightest emotional deviation is sure to register as brightly as when the bombs fell. Oh for founders' sake, I actually redlined. And this time it will count towards my ranking. *Breathe in for six, hold for six, out for six.*

'Where am I on the leaderboard?'

'It doesn't matter right now.'

I feel a wave of something course through my body without warning, and I'm too late to stop it. It feels surprisingly liberating. The machine glows brightly and Sia gazes at me.

'I need you to operate,' I say.

'I'm sorry, Eve.'

And then I understand. It's the overseers. They are deliberately jeopardising my chances at the harvest by refusing the procedure. Maybe that's what happened to Luc, too, and that's why they have enlisted Sam to watch me and goad me into feeling.

'The overseers don't want me to pass, do they?' I say, feeling my eyes prickle with tears.

'Don't be silly, Eve. You just have a sickness.' She folds the screen in half and leans it against the machine on the table.

There, she confirmed it. I *am* sick. I try to remember the names of the illnesses from before so I can work out which one I have. There was cancer, and the flu, and heart disease. Do I have one of those sicknesses, perhaps?

'I ran some tests, and it appears that the sickness you have is an emotional one. The physical reactions you are experiencing are simply by-products.'

What are some of the emotional sicknesses we have been taught about? Greed. Violence. Addiction. Vanity. I can recall the words, but they mean nothing to me, and I can't even begin to remember the symptoms. I suppose I didn't pay enough attention in those classes, and I make a mental note to study up on the illnesses of the *old world* before the harvest.

'You have a sickness called grief.'

'Grief,' I repeat; trying, and failing, to conjure up my mental notes on the term. The medic picks her flexi-screen up again, types into it, and then hands it to me. I scan the words.

Illness: Grief

An emotional response to loss. Characterised by a feeling of sadness or despair, individuals suffering from grief may experience a range of physical and psychological symptoms.

I glance through the list of symptoms and feel myself relax. For some reason, being able to put a name to the sickness is oddly comforting. I don't know how I contracted the illness, but that doesn't matter anyway; I'm sure that there is a pill to fix it. What really matters is getting better, and being back on track with the harvest. That must be why the overseers couldn't operate on me – you can't operate on a sick person. I take back all of my critical thoughts about them.

'I can help you to get better, Eve, but first, we must work out why you have this illness, and I'm afraid you might not like my hypothesis.'

'Oh.' My body feels extremely heavy, and I wonder if I am going to slip back to sleep.

'As you have probably worked out, the catalyst for the grief sickness was Luc being culled.' The machine beside me blips, and I glare at it. 'The thing is, Eve, people are culled all the time, and every now and then – not often, but every now and then – people do react in this way.'

'They do?'

'Oh, yes. Near the end of each cycle, and particularly on the lead up to the harvest, every guardian knows that they need to be prepared for their dependant to be culled. But sometimes their minds aren't strong enough. It's all documented in the Book of Eridu. Of course, there's been less of an issue since we worked out how to communicate with people on the Grid instead. Most people are able to accept it, but not you, for some reason. What is your aversion to the Grid?'

I just shrug. So it's my fault that I am suffering from this grief sickness. My mind just isn't strong enough. I gaze at the half-open door on the far side of the room; did I just see a shadow move behind it, or am I totally losing the plot?

'And in your case, Luc was so high up on the leaderboard that you must have just taken it for granted that he would succeed in the harvest.'

I don't trust myself to speak. It feels like if I open my mouth, more than just words will tumble out of me. Instead, I just nod my head.

'The problem is, you have been suffering from a different illness for a long time, one we should have diagnosed a lot earlier, but never detected.'

'I was? What sort of sickness? I didn't feel sick.' The shadow in the doorway moves again and I tear my gaze away from it. It is probably just another test.

'This sickness was most likely the most dangerous of all in the *old world*. It was called love.'

I don't need her to show me the screen this time. Love is one of those illnesses that we all tut-tut about and shake our heads.

Love: A strong bond between two people.

People fought, and died, and destroyed the world, often in the name of love. I can't believe I was suffering from an illness and I didn't even know. I remember what Sam said, about being lucky to have the bond with my brother. Yeah right, lucky.

'You were very good at concealing the illness, I think you even hid it from yourself. The thing is, Eve, all the other students have had to work at controlling their emotions. They felt them, and then they suppressed them; they slowly learnt to cope with the tests. You, however, were different.'

Sia sits on the edge of the bed.

'You probably felt emotions early on in the preschool, before you had a monitor to alert the overseers. But you were a smart girl, and you learnt quickly. You still are, and it isn't only your emotional control that has you consistently at the top of the leaderboard. The problem is that now that you have been faced with a crisis, with your brother being culled, you haven't learnt how to cope with the new wave of emotions accosting you, not like the others did. You have never felt them, not properly, instead you just detached yourself from, well… yourself. If you wish to stay at the top of the leaderboard, you need to learn, and quickly.'

Sia looks over at the machine making little whirring sounds beside me. I feel my eyes prickle with wetness. It's one of those grief symptoms. 'So what now?'

'I could be wrong, but there is the possibility that now that you have allowed your body to feel some strong emotions, that more could be coming. First grief, then perhaps anger, maybe fear. The door has been opened, just a crack, and now anything can come through.'

I feel sick. I don't want to experience any of these things, I just want to go back to feeling numb.

'You need to shut that door again, Eve, and lock it tight.'

'The pills, the Lortnok? They helped.' My voice sounds panicked. 'Something happened to my prescriptions…'

'Ah, yes. We are always learning here, you see. Always improving. Unfortunately, there are those who believe the Lortnok does more harm than good.'

I shake my head, trying to communicate the fact that I want – need – that additional support.

'The problem with the Lortnok is that it suppresses the emotions *for* you. It isn't really you, now is it? And the more you take it, the higher the dose you need in order to feel the same effects. Eventually, it's just not going to work at all.'

I want to tell her that I don't care if it's not me learning to suppress emotions. I don't care if I have to take six or eight or ten pills a day. I just want the emotions to go away so that I can stay at the top of the leaderboard. The leaderboard… I haven't had a chance to find my flexi-screen and see where I am on the list, but after redlining yesterday and being absent from the institute for a full day of classes, I know that I won't be at the top anymore. I try to approach this thought with an air of calm indifference, but it's hard. The beeping from the machine beside my bed increases in both pitch and intensity.

'I am sure the architects are doing all they can to ensure that you are prepared for the harvest,' says Sia.

Yes, I'm sure they are.

There is a knock on the door and I look up, wondering if it's going to be my guardians, or perhaps Hana, or one of the elite.

It's Sam.

'What are you doing here?'

He doesn't seem taken aback by my tone of voice, but Sia looks at me sharply and I remind myself I need to be on my best behaviour.

'Nice to see you too, Eve.' He smiles and pulls a seat up next to my bed.

Sia looks at my charts one last time. 'Your guardians will be here to take you back to Block A soon. I'll have some food sent up.'

And with that, she turns to leave. 'I shouldn't have visitors, should I, Sia? I mean, I'm sick.'

But she just shrugs. 'It's fine. It's not the type of sickness you can catch.' She leaves the room and Sam gazes at me, making me feel uncomfortable. I wonder why he is here, what is the point.

'So, you finally felt something, didn't you?'

'Go away.'

I roll over onto my side and close my eyes.

'Admit it, Eve. You are finally turning into a human.'

'Not the type of human that they want in Eridu,' I retort. 'Get culled.'

He laughs, and my monitor goes amber as I imagine throttling him. I try to relax, but it isn't working, not with him sitting there goading me.

'If you're just going to sit there, how about you explain to me why you don't have a monitor.'

'Curiosity isn't a desired virtue,' he says, and I ball my hands up into fists so that my nails are cutting into my palms. It makes me feel a little better, but then I've had enough. I sit up in the bed, and my monitor is glowing crimson. The machine beside my bed lights up like the large lights on the ceiling of the open spaces in Eridu. I look directly at him, not even trying to keep the emotion out of my voice. If I've redlined once, I suddenly don't care if I do it again.

'Why do you hate me so much,' I begin, my voice quavering. 'What have I done that makes you want me to get culled? To go to the Grid? To end my life here? It's not going to benefit you in any way, so why do you keep doing it?'

'I don't hate you,' he says, feigning surprise.

'Well what, then? Is this all just a game to you? I don't even know why they let you in here. You're destined for the Grid, but I might actually have a chance, you know?'

Something dark drops off the ceiling of the roof and lands in my lap. I stare at the spider, but I'm already redlining, so I don't even attempt to push my revulsion away. There's no point trying to flick it off; that's not how the hallucinations work. Instead, I roll back onto my side and close my eyes tightly. I'm not sure how long he sits there, but he doesn't try to speak to me again, thank goodness, and after a while I descend into a fitful sleep.

XX

As I expected, the redline drops me a long way down the leaderboard. My guardians barely look at me as we walk back through the tunnel to Block A. What must they be thinking? Last time that I redlined we all just pretended that it didn't happen. This time, there is no possibility of ignoring it.

As we walk through A-Tunnel, I see the words from the Book of Eridu drifting overhead and make up my mind. After all, we are supposed to share any concerns with our guardians so that they can guide us to walk in the path of the founders.

'Can I ask a question?' I say at last.

'Of course,' says my prime, and my sec nods.

'Is it about the harvest?' she asks.

I wonder if you get an instruction manual when you become a guardian. Perhaps there's a list of common questions and appropriate responses. *If your dependant approaches you in the final cycle, it is probably because she is concerned about the harvest. Appropriate responses listed below.*

'It's not about the harvest,' I say. 'I was just… It's about the incident.'

We walk through one of the little pools of light and I can just make out my prime's face. It is blank, as always.

'It's disappointing, of course,' says my sec. 'But I'm sure you will be back on top of the leaderboard in no time.'

Does she really think that I can recover from a redline? 'No, not about me,' I say. 'I'm talking about the *other* incident. I'm just wondering how you are coping.'

I say it carefully, lightly, so as not to be misconstrued.

'Really, Eve, you need to be a little more specific.'

Do I? Are there so many awful incidents in our lives that it is impossible to work out which one I am possibly referring to? But then again, it's an odd question, I suppose. They are coping just fine because they are following the virtues. I should just leave it, and yet...

I take a deep breath.

'The incident where Luc was culled.'

The silence stretches out before me like the dark tunnel. What do I want them to say? Do I want them to reiterate the virtues and tell me that we must be content with all that has passed and all that is yet to come? Or would I rather that one of them admits that they have experienced a strong emotion since Luc left. That I'm not alone with my feelings, and with my sickness.

My sec finally speaks. 'Luc?'

My stomach sinks.

'You go on ahead,' says my prime and my sec nods and hurries along to the end of the tunnel and out into the light. My prime turns to me.

'I don't want you to talk about Luc in front of your sec again.'

I nod. I should have guessed that she would have undergone the memrase procedure. I feel a brief tinge of jealousy, wishing that I, too, could be so oblivious as to what happened in the past.

'I understand.' We have stopped between two pools of light so I can't see the expression on my prime's face. Not that I need to; it would be perfectly sculptured into a look of indifference. 'But what about you?' I push him. 'How are you coping?'

'Eve,' says my prime, running a hand through his short, dark hair. 'Luc may not be here with us physically any more, but he will always be with us.'

I nod, thinking of the way I was able to speak to my grand-guardian.

'You should be content. He may not have been worthy to stay in Eridu, but now he is immortal, living on the Grid. Try to see the positives.'

'Prime,' I say quietly, aware that we are completely alone in the tunnel. The glow of my monitor illuminates the wall slightly with a tinge of blue. 'Is it really him?'

My prime sighs, and the sound is swallowed up by the darkness. 'I already explained to you that what you saw at the transfer chambers that time was simply a physical reaction. The shells sometimes struggle to let go. Just like you are struggling to let go of Luc.'

I don't think it's a very good analogy. Turning, I keep walking towards the light at the end of the tunnel. If I am culled – which is a given, if I keep redlining – will my shell, too, struggle to let go? And will I care at all, if my essence is already on the way to the Grid to spend eternity with my brother?

Will it really be me, or just a copy – my real essence disintegrating along with my shell?

'We will be moving tomorrow after your duties,' says my prime.

Moving? Of course, moving to the multi. Our unit will be reallocated to a family whose dependant is higher up on the ladder than me. I haven't been in the multi since joining the ranked. No, earlier than that; my guardians and I moved into a unit when Luc was first old enough to be ranked, and he was a cycle ahead of me.

I don't answer, and we reach the end of the tunnel and emerge into the courtyard in front of Block A.

'I'm sure we'll be back soon enough.'

My prime talks for a while about strategies to cope with the tests. He tells me nothing I don't already know, and I tell him that I'm tired, that I need to go to my pod.

'Of course,' says my prime. 'Sleep well.'

I try not to think about the next family unit that moves in, unaware of the significance of the steel bracket clinging to the wall beneath one of the pods.

We have searched in vain, but so far there are only six of us. That's not enough to save humanity, is it? What are we going to do?

Book of Eridu

XXI

The next morning, my guardians are waiting for me when I emerge from my pod. Of course they are, they will be keeping a close eye on me from now on.

'How did you sleep?' my prime asks, but I know that he can see all of my data on his own flexi-screen.

'Fine,' I lie. I have the peculiar sensation of falling, of my stomach twisting up inside and the skin all over my body prickling uncomfortably. I close my eyes and remember what I learnt in the emotional control classes.

When I open my eyes, my sec is staring hard at a spot on the cool concrete floor. I don't bother asking how she slept. She has her flexi-screen clasped in her hand and I can see the leaderboard on the front.

'I'll do some more exercise tonight,' I suggest, but they are both silent. 'Right, well I'm going to get ready for the institute.'

'Rank well,' says my prime, but he doesn't sound quite as optimistic as yesterday.

I meet Lil in the passage on the way to the communal hall.

'I can't talk to you,' she says, moving briskly along the corridor.

She's seen the leaderboard then. Who am I kidding, of course she has; everyone will have seen the leaderboard by now.

'Well good morning to you, too.'

'I'm serious. You're redlining, Eve. It's not a good idea for me to hang around with you.'

I hurry to keep up with her, and am reminded of the way I

131

spoke to Hana just recently. Is this what she felt like?

'Eve, you'd cut me off if you were in the same position.'

She's right, but I'm not going to give her the satisfaction of confirming it.

'Look,' I begin, 'it was a once off, okay? It won't happen again.'

'It wasn't a once off.' Lil turns abruptly and I nearly walk into her. She lowers her voice so that I have to lean in to hear her. 'Emotions are dangerous. You know that. Now stay away from me.'

As I walk into the communal hall, I stare out at all the people sitting at the tables. Today, the merging of colours seems overwhelming, rather than relaxing.

Although I'm standing behind her, Lil doesn't talk to me at all in the nutrition line. My eyes follow her as she collects her food and joins the elite. There is still one seat left over at the table; perhaps the others are giving me a second chance after all.

'Scan your ID, please.'

I turn to see that it's Polee serving breakfast this morning. I glance back over at the group of elite. Yes, I'm right. The empty seat is Polee's and there's a new person sitting at the table. The status quo has changed, and I am no part of this new social order. I am falling.

I scan my ID card and Polee turns to retrieve my vitamins for the morning. As she hands them to me, I notice that she doesn't make eye contact.

I glance over the food on offer.

'A banana and some oats, thanks.'

'Bananas are in short supply, only for those at the top of the leaderboard.'

'Are you serious?'

Of course she's serious. When you spend your life with a high ranking, you don't even realise the little luxuries you are afforded; bananas for breakfast, a private room… they just seem normal.

'That's fine, just some oats thanks.'

The oxy-creds are deducted and I collect my breakfast tray, looking around for somewhere to sit. Hana catches my gaze but I avert my eyes. I can't ignore the way the boy sitting next to her frowns and says something to her. I'm too far away to hear what he is saying, but I can imagine. Don't invite her over here, she's redlining.

I spy an empty table over at the side of the room and make my way towards it instead. I'm sure Hana has redlined in the past, but then again, perhaps not. Feeling a strong emotion usually comes across as amber. For the monitor to go red there has to be a full-on freak-out of epic proportions.

Yep, that's me.

If I was concerned about everybody staring and whispering, I am soon proven wrong. Instead, it's as though I'm not there, just a ghostly wisp that people can see straight through. It's like I already have one foot in the Grid. Perhaps I do.

I sit with my back to the leaderboard so I don't have to be constantly reminded of my failings. I try to tell myself that it's not the end of the world, and that I just need to remember my training so I can somehow move back up the ladder. But who am I kidding?

My eyes rest on Sam, who is sitting by himself a couple of tables over, and I feel some emotion bubble beneath the surface. Anger, I think. I close my eyes, breathing deeply, attempting to calm my rapidly beating heart.

'Hi, Eve.'

I just about let out a groan, but manage to stop myself. I open my eyes to see Sam slipping into the seat opposite me. He really can't take a hint.

'How are you feeling today?' he asks.

'As if you care.'

His eyes travel down my arm to my monitor, which isn't quite at amber yet, but it's close.

'Breathe, Eve,' he says gently.

'Get culled.' But I do take a deep breath, focusing my thoughts, and my monitor pales. I pick up my spoon and begin to eat my breakfast.

'Look, I'm sorry for pushing you yesterday,' he says. 'Really, it was uncalled for.'

I stare at my bowl of oats. I have bigger things to worry about than Sam.

'So I suppose you will be sitting with me during mealtimes, now?' he asks.

'Yeah, right. I might have redlined, but at least I'm actually *on* the board.'

Sam smiles, and I can't help noticing once again how easily it comes to him. 'I've got something to show you.'

He seems excited, and as he pushes the sleeve of his jumpsuit back, I can see the newly implanted monitor on his wrist, pulsing amber. Oh, Sam, you're already mucking it up.

'Congratulations,' I say, hollowly.

'And…' He turns slightly, pushing a few light strands of hair aside to show the sticky dot adhered to the side of his neck, behind his ear. 'Ta-da.'

I want to explain to him that the stim isn't exactly something to be excited about, but I suppose there is no point now. He will soon figure that out for himself.

'That's great, Sam. Enjoy.'

He seems confused at my tone, but surely he realises that a

quick apology isn't enough to make up for the part he played in making me feel emotions. For making me redline. Okay, that's probably unfair, it was more the medic's doing, or whoever is responsible for not allowing me to have the Lortnok.

'Look, unless you're here to explain why you weren't on the leaderboard and why you didn't have a monitor until today, then I'm not exactly interested in whatever you have to say to me. I need to focus on getting better; on getting my emotions back under control.'

Sam looks at me for a moment, and I wonder if he is going to take his tray and move back over to his seat. Good riddance if he does.

'I can tell you,' he says at last, his voice low. 'But not yet.'

'When?'

He shrugs. 'Later.'

'Later when? Later today? Later next week? Later after we've both been culled.'

It's the first time I've seriously entertained the thought of possibly being culled, and it fills me with dread.

'That's very dramatic.'

My monitor pulses with a brighter blue. For founders' sake.

Sam stares off behind me at the leaderboard. Informer? Ladder climber? Mentally impaired?

'I'm not sure when I can tell you. Sometime soon.'

'You really need to get that under control,' I say, nodding at his monitor, and he gazes at the thin band as it transitions from blue, to amber, to blue, to amber like a shorting light. 'Do you really feel that many emotions?'

'I'd never really thought about it,' he says, openly fascinated. 'But I guess I'll be sitting here, and then I'll think of something funny, or sad, or I'll get excited.' He looks over at my monitor, which I've managed to keep blue. Just. 'How do you stop yourself feeling so much?'

It's my turn to shrug. 'Practice.' I finish the last bite of my breakfast. 'See you at the institute.'

The founders saw that the world was doomed, and the fate of humanity as well. So they dreamed of a new world, and they called it Eridu.

Book of Eridu

XXII

I haven't taken the long route between Block A and the institute since before the harvest ceremony. However, after redlining yesterday, the memories encased within the longer path seem to be calling out to me across time. Besides, I don't exactly feel like walking along A-Tunnel with all the other students, watching their eyes gaze straight through me as though I'm not there. The only person who seemed to notice me this morning was Sam, and he's not exactly the desired type of acquaintance.

I walk through the courtyard and turn left into the lesser-used C-Tunnel. At first, I can see very little, as my eyes struggle to adjust from the bright lights out in the courtyard. But slowly, slowly, the patterns that line the ceiling fade into view. This tunnel isn't covered with words, like A-Tunnel, and the remnants of my memories collide painfully with the present.

'What are those white things?' I had asked my guardians when I was still young enough not to know better. The pale shapes plastered oddly on the roof of the tunnel looked alien, and despite their innocent curves, strangely threatening to my six-year-old-mind.

'Curiosity is not a desired virtue,' my primary guardian had reprimanded me, but Luc had simply smiled.

'Those were called clouds,' he told me, ignoring the looks he was getting from our guardians.

'Clouds.' I tried the unfamiliar word on my tongue, and then moved closer to the protection of my secondary guardian's warm body. 'Have you ever seen a real cloud, Mama?'

My sec had frowned at Luc. 'You need to stop reading her those stories from the *old world*. It's not appropriate for her to call me that.'

Luc had crouched down in front of me, his eyes brown and warm. 'There are no clouds anymore, Evie.'

'Good,' I had responded, suppressing a small shiver.

'But you can't call our sec 'Mama,' because she isn't and you know it. If the overseers hear you say that...'

His voice had trailed off, but even at six years old I knew that I didn't want to be on the radar of the overseers. It had been a deliberate choice, to call her that, as I'd wanted to see how she would react. I liked the sound of it. Mama. It sounded warmer than 'sec,' which was simply an abbreviation of her title, secondary guardian. Of course, she wasn't really my mother anyway. The founders are the parents of us all, and my prime and sec were simply my guardians, chosen to fulfil their duties for the founders of Eridu.

These days, eleven years on, many of the cloud paintings have begun to peel, flaking fragments of white paint onto the floor of the tunnel. It's ironic, really, that a reproduction of a world that has disintegrated is now also falling apart. I'm not sure who painted the clouds; perhaps the founders – who else would bother replicating something that no longer existed unless out of nostalgia for a life they had once known. Then again, Luc and I were endlessly fascinated with the *old world*, far more than anybody else I'd talked to in Eridu. Perhaps if we were tasked with the job of painting images on a tunnel…

I think of the other tunnels in Eridu. Some of them have paintings, too, but most are newer than the cloud tunnel and depict the six virtues or the mottos of Eridu. Will the overseers replace the clouds when they have finally all flaked onto the ground? Probably not. It's more likely that they will update C-Tunnel to reflect a more modern sentiment.

Reaching a split in C-Tunnel, I turn left and take the rougher, barely used H-tunnel which heads directly towards the outer wall of Eridu. C-Tunnel might not be used that often, but compared to H-Tunnel it is a multi-lane highway. Whereas C-Tunnel is smooth and worn, H-Tunnel is a rough-hewn pathway through still-jagged rock jutting out into the passage. I'm not sure if it was dug out by hand or by rudimentary machines, but either way, it is clearly much older than any of the other tunnels in Eridu. It is darker, too, with fewer fluorescent lights lining the ceiling and no paintings of any kind.

I sometimes think that H-Tunnel is the closest I will ever get to the *old world*. In Eridu, everything is monitored and scheduled and controlled. All except for the clouds peeling off C-Tunnel and the jagged rocks of H-Tunnel. Why did the overseers leave it like this? Perhaps it is just a reminder of why we should be thankful for Eridu. And besides, hardly anybody walks this way so it would be a waste of resources to fix it up.

Luc and I used to walk this way to school sometimes, when we had the time. At first, I found it disconcerting the way the rough tunnel walls reached downwards like gnarled hands, but Luc had taught me not to be scared.

I can see him now, in my mind's eye, speaking easily with me as we walked the long way to the institute.

'You know, there's a trick to staying at the top of the leaderboard,' he had told me.

'What's that?'

He had knelt down, for, despite only being a year older than me, he had grown taller much more quickly. 'You have to imagine that it's a dream, or that you are standing outside yourself watching what is going on. Try it, next time. You simply separate your mind from your body, and then nothing can ever touch you or concern you again.'

I sigh, and continue along the tunnel. I will allow myself, just once, to hear the ghosts of the past. After this, I won't take this pathway again. I need to put the harvest, and the culled, out of my mind.

Nearing the outer wall, I find my pace slowing, until I finally stop at the place where the pathway takes a sudden turn and angles sharply back across the compound towards the institute. It is as though the creators of the tunnel miscalculated, realising that they were heading in the wrong direction and were about to reach the boundary of Eridu.

I can't remember the last time I walked this way. Luc became preoccupied with preparing for the harvest in his final cycle, and Lil didn't see the point in taking the longer route; particularly a longer, darker, less-used route where the rocks looked like hands. This spot, where the tunnel changes angles, also opens up so that I can see the outer wall, and the secret encased there. Although it is the closest I can get to the wall without climbing over the metal barriers, I am still a long way from that rough grey surface. I long to get closer, to run my hands along the wall and to feel the raised edges of the faded markings left by the founders. There are letters and numbers inscribed there which mean nothing at all to me, or seemingly to anyone else for that matter.

And there, nestled in the base of the wall, lies a secret. It isn't exactly hidden, per se. Perhaps that is the thing with secrets; the best ones are hidden in plain sight. It is the same grey colour as the rest of the outer wall and so it blends in unless you know what you are looking for. Luc had been the first one to point it out, telling me to notice the slight change in texture, the raised circle protruding from the middle.

And how *he* had noticed it, I will probably never know. Slowly, slowly my eyes had worked out what he was showing me. A small door nestled in the base of the wall, with a round five-spoked handle in the middle. It was all painted the same grey colour as the walls.

'What's behind it?' I had asked, knowing that he was the one person in Eridu who wouldn't reprimand me for being curious. But he had just shrugged, smiling.

Now that I'm older, I am well aware that it is probably nothing interesting anyway. Maybe it is an old maintenance door which leads to the air ducts and the machines maintaining the oxygen levels. Or perhaps the waste that can't be used to make paper, or clothes, or turned into fertiliser ends up behind that door. Part of me would like to imagine that it leads to the surface, but the thought also scares me in some abstract way. Most importantly, it reminds me of Luc, and even though he is gone it's like some little secret that we still have; a link to each other. Maybe it leads to the Grid.

I shake myself. I've given myself enough time to remember him. If I want to pass the harvest then I need to put him out of my mind.

Like a city that is broken down and without walls, is a man whose spirit is without restraint.

Book of Eridu

XXIII

The school day passes smoothly enough. I ace my academic tests, but then again, the academic aspects of the institute were never the problem. I claw my way up a couple of places, but when you're that far down the ladder, moving up a couple of positions doesn't mean much at all.

Inside the classrooms, I can almost pretend that nothing has changed. It's the same droning voices of the professors; the same students sitting at the same desks. Nobody talks to me, but that's because we are all very busy, of course. I fool myself into believing that I'm the same person I was yesterday.

It's lunchtime when the impact of redlining really starts to sink in. There are pockets of students that I could attempt to sit with, those who are low-ranked, but I've never really interacted with them before so it seems impossible to start now. I doubt that Hana would protest, but I am reminded of the way that I pushed her away over the years. No, I would feel like less of an outsider if I was sitting by myself.

Just as I'm putting my lunch tray down, Sam looks up from his book and beckons me over. I could ignore him – I *should* ignore him – but instead I just sigh and move over to sit opposite him. If he's an informer then surely he's already got all of the information he needs by now, anyway.

'Are you still reading that thing?' I say, indicating the book in his hands.

'I'm a slow reader. Have you read it?'

'The Book of Eridu? There's no need. The professors teach us all that we need to know in class. It would be a waste of time to…' I look at Sam, and then change tack. 'I just think there are better uses of my time.'

'Things sound different when out of context.' There is a strange tone in his voice but I just shrug.

'Fair enough, but I'm sure our professors can interpret it better than we can anyway.'

'Perhaps.' Sam closes the book and puts it aside on the table, and I become aware of how similar we are now. Two outsiders in Eridu, but for different reasons. I wonder if it is easier for him, always having been low-ranked, than it is for me. After all, I know what it's like at the top, so I'm aware of what I'm missing out on.

'I mean, the Book was written by six people,' I continue, 'with six different views of what was happening in those first few cycles. I've heard that it's like reading a bunch of disjointed diary entries and digging through the rocks looking for gemstones.'

'I suppose it is sort of like that,' he admits, 'but it's still interesting. Did you know that nobody passed the first harvest?'

I think back to what I had been taught about the first few cycles. 'Are you sure?'

'Yep, well it says so in there.' He nods at the book. 'Year ten: First harvest. Success rate: zero per cent.'

'Ten,' I repeat, taking a bite of my sandwich. 'Well, that was their problem. Nobody would be able to succeed in the harvest at ten, that's why we wait until seventeen.'

'Eve, what actually happens in the harvest?'

'Tests,' I reply, swallowing my mouthful. 'Academic, physical, and emotional. There's a range of others that are assessed throughout the cycles as well. Leadership. Patriotism. Only the best remain in Eridu.'

'So are you telling me,' he leans forward slightly, 'that in the first harvest nobody was good enough to stay in Eridu? All of the children went to the Grid?'

'Well, I suppose if that's what it says in there, then it's true.'

'Yeah.' He ponders this for a moment, and then changes the subject. 'Hey watch this.'

Sam pulls the sleeve of his jumpsuit up and lays his arm on the table. It is glowing a cool blue. I almost smile at how proud of himself he is, but quickly stop myself. Anybody could be watching.

'Come on,' he says, 'do you know how long it took me to get it staying this way? I've been practising all morning.'

Hardly noticing what I'm doing, I push the sleeve of my own jumpsuit up and lay my arm next to his on the table, so our monitors are lying next to each other, glowing the same hue of blue. My arm lightly touches his, and I feel the hairs on the back of my arm prickle slightly.

'We used to play a game when we were kids,' I explain. 'To see who could stay blue the longest. We'd try everything to make the other person feel something. Tell scary stories, make them laugh, get someone else to walk up behind them and give them a fright.'

His light blue eyes look straight into my own. 'Let me guess, you won every time.'

'Yep.'

He laughs and his bracelet glows a brighter blue, tinged slightly with streaks of amber. He frowns, concentrating, and the bracelet returns to a light blue. He looks quite satisfied with himself.

'See, I'm getting better at this.'

I wonder again how somebody can get to seventeen years of age without controlling their emotions, and without having a monitor. But we shouldn't talk somewhere like this, out in the open. It'll need to wait.

'They say that before the harvest, you felt nothing,' says Sam, carefully.

'Who says that?'

'Everybody.'

I shrug. 'I found it easy.'

'And you don't find it so easy anymore?'

Our monitors pulse in time with each other, pale blue, while I think of the leaderboard. 'Clearly.'

'Tell me, were you happy with not feeling anything?'

I raise an eyebrow. 'Of course. The past few days have been… disappointing. And now, even if I remain blue for the rest of the cycle, I know that it's impossible for me to re-join the elite. That means there's no possibility at all of being harvested for a premium position, and there is a greater risk of being culled.' I think of my grand-guardian forever encased within a screen.

'But even if you were in the elite, that's no guarantee that you'd be okay, right?'

'Sam,' I say carefully, determined not to say my brother's name aloud. 'In all seventeen years of my life, I've only ever seen one person in the elite fail the harvest.'

Sam reaches across the table and touches my hand lightly. I am reminded of the spider that fell from the roof of the hospital, but I suppress the urge to move away.

'Don't you feel anything?' he asks.

'I feel your fingers on my hand.'

My monitor is a cool blue, but Sam's is starting to pulse brightly. I remove myself from my body.

'Why do you do that?' he asks, voice low.

'Do what?'

'One moment you're here, with me. And the next you are

somewhere else.'

I ignore his touch, and stare off into the distance. 'It's the way I learnt to stop feeling.'

He releases me, and I instantly relax.

'Emotions aren't all that bad, you know,' says Sam.

'Of course they are,' I reply, looking around to see if anyone has heard him. Nobody is close enough, thankfully.

'They aren't,' he says again.

'You only think emotions aren't bad because you don't know how to suppress them,' I explain. 'It's your way of legitimising your failures.'

'Gee, say it how you mean it, Eve.'

'It's true. There's this kid in my class who was never very good at biology. So he told himself that biology wasn't very useful anyway, that there was no point. You are doing the same thing.'

He looks at me. 'Or perhaps I truly believe that some emotions are okay. That emotions are what make us human.'

I shake my head. 'Then you're wrong. Emotions are the antithesis of humanity. Emotions led to humankind virtually wiping themselves out.'

'Ourselves.'

'What?'

'You said *themselves*. We are humans too, or have you forgotten that?'

I think about telling him that I don't want to know why he didn't have a monitor after all. That curiosity is not a desired virtue in Eridu, and that I want to uphold all of the virtues like I have for the past seventeen years. I don't want to be culled.

But the words stick in my throat.

'I've got a question for you,' says Sam, opening up the Book of Eridu again. He finds the page he is after and turns it around to show me. I can see tables of numbers and results colliding together on the thin paper. 'What's this all about?'

I scan down the page. It looks like harvest results and yet…

'Oh, I think it's just data on the children from the first cycle.' I flick forward in the book, noting how fragile the paper feels beneath my fingers. The Book of Eridu in this form is far less cohesive than what we have in our flexi-screens. There are snippets of words and phrases written in the margins, and numbers and grids scattered throughout the pages. 'Here, look.' I tap my finger on another list. 'It's similar to how we measure different factors in the incubation chambers. I'm not sure on all the things they were measuring, but the numbers down the side look familiar. Have you worked at the incubation chambers before?'

Sam shakes his head.

'It's probably because you're not high-ranked. Next time I'm rostered on, if you don't have a duty at the same time you should come with me.'

'Okay, sure.'

I close the book and slip it back across the table to him, trying not to think about the fact that now I'm low-ranked too.

XXIV

When I get back to Block A after school, my guardians and I move our belongings into the multi; it only takes one trip. The multi is just a large room, really, with pods stacked high up above each other, supported by metal rods. In a way, the glistening towers of metal remind me of the exo-wombs. It's not as quiet and peaceful as the incubation chambers, however, with swarms of people moving around the space rather than floating in hushed tranquillity.

There is no privacy in the multi, with everyone shoved together in the same space. There are shared desks around the edges of the room, and shared bathroom facilities as well. Even the oxy-creds we generate from the plants around the walls are divided up between us all, and I'm just thankful that we have so many banked up already, so that I won't have to go without. The oxy-creds aren't only deducted for meals, but for school resources and use of the leisure facilities as well. It's hard to imagine growing up in the multi all your life.

My guardians' faces are blank, but I can tell that they aren't completely content with the change of scenery. That's the point though, isn't it, for moving the low-ranked to the multi. To limit their – our – privileges and drive a wedge between the groups. I used to think that it just made sense that those who worked harder received the best food, accommodation, and positions in Eridu. But it's not really true, is it? It's a bit of a fallacy that hard work automatically equals the best results.

I worked hard, of course, throughout all my years at the institute, but did I really work harder than these low-ranked students? Emotional control always came so naturally to me, that at times it almost seemed like my monitor was frozen on blue. The only place I had to work hard to stay indifferent was in the transfer centre, and even then that was only three or four cycles ago, after I saw the screaming shell.

From the top of the ladder, the inequalities between the ranks seemed like motivation. If you too, work hard, you can have all of this. But from the bottom, it appears a little different.

After I have stacked my school books on a small shelf allocated to me, I gaze around the room, wondering where Hana's pod is, or perhaps Sam's. I walk along the narrow path between the pods, crisscrossing from one side of the multi to the other, looking up at the ladders stretching towards the ceiling.

The areas of the multi are divided up by cohort so I know the general vicinity in which I should find them. I see a flash of red hair and turn – Hana's pod is there, over to the left, near the wall. I consider going over to say hello, but my feet grow roots and adhere me to the foor. What would I say? Hi, Hana, I know I've avoided you for so long, but now that I'm redlining I was wondering if we could be friends?

I keep walking, looking around for Sam instead. I can't see him, and I soon give up; there are too many pods and my brain is too tired to distinguish between one low-ranked student and another. Besides, perhaps he has duties, or he's at the gym, or has already curled up and gone to sleep. The last option sounds like a plan.

I turn on my heel and walk back towards my own pod, third up from the floor. My prime is sitting in the base of his pod, working on his flexi-screen. He looks up as I arrive.

'I'm going to go to sleep,' I say to him.

He nods. 'Have you done your exercise?'

I hesitate. 'I'll do double tomorrow.'

In the past, my prime probably wouldn't have minded, but things are different now that I'm redlining.

'No, you won't.'

I sigh, but he's probably right; the exercise will help me sleep. I collect a towel and a spare jumpsuit and make my way to the gym, aware that my prime is watching me every step of the way.

When I enter the gym, the first thing I notice is that all of the treadmills have been taken. Damn. There is a row of brown and grey jumpsuits, unranked and ranked, running along at a brisk pace. I hesitate for a moment, wondering if any of them are nearly finished. Polee walks past me, bumping into me slightly, and walks directly up to one of the treadmills, leaning past the student and pushing a button on their flexi-screen. The treadmill loses power so that the student's pace slows and finally stops.

They don't complain, of course, because Polee is in the elite. As I contemplate some of the other equipment, a student on the end treadmill slows their pace as well, and so I walk over, not realising who it is until I get closer.

'Oh, hey, Sam. Are you nearly done here?'

His pace slows to a walk and finally, he stops, sweat glistening on his skin. 'Yeah sure, go for it.'

He removes his flexi-screen and I put my own one in, activating the exercise program.

'So you're all moved into the multi?'

'Yep. Whereabouts is your pod?' I set the machine to start off at a brisk walk.

'Oh, I'm not in the multi.'

I look across at him, but he is mopping his face with a towel so I can't see his facial expression.

'You're kidding, right?'

'No, I'm in a unit. Number 32.'

'Are you serious? Why?'

He shrugs. 'I suppose the overseers felt sorry for me, being at the bottom and all.'

That's not the way it works, and he knows it.

'Sam, are you like the dependant of a past overseer or something? Why do you have so many privileges?'

I know that overseers don't generally partner or raise children, but if they did…

'I'll tell you at some stage. Anyway, see you around.'

I put all my energy into running for as long and fast as I can, sweating out thoughts and feelings though my pores.

***

It starts with a noise. Just a light tapping which comes from the outside of my pod.

Cocooned in the darkness, I keep my eyes firmly closed, hoping that the sound is nothing more than the wispy tendrils of my dream slipping inadvertently into the waking world.

The visions that plagued me overnight had certainly been strange, but now that I try to remember them they quickly scurry away into the darkness. Something about a river from the *old world,* and a garden, but the garden was made of wires all twisted up and pulsing with an odd blue light.

I give up, and then the sound comes again.

Tap, tap, tap.

The sound wasn't a dream, then. For founders' sake.

151

Sighing, I push the rough blanket down to my waist and the soft blue glow of the monitor illuminates a small section of the otherwise darkened pod. In the gently pulsing light, I can just make out the rounded side of the pod; smooth and arching into a low roof above me. A pale section of the roof glows blue barely two feet above my body. And there, nestled above me, lies my flexi-screen - currently dark and dormant.

It's basically the same as the pod in my unit, although it seems like it may be an earlier model. I press a button on the side of the monitor and a series of glowing digits wink innocently up at me. 2145. I stifle a yawn. It is odd for the architects to wake us so late, but on the other hand, it is clear that during the final cycle, all semblance of normality is quickly disappearing like the culled on harvest day.

I know that I can't ignore the tapping sound for long, but I still hesitate for a moment in the darkness, collecting my thoughts. Breathing deeply, I try to instil a calm sense of security in my mind. *Breathe in for six, hold for six, out for six.* 'Like a city that is broken down and without walls,' I whisper the familiar words into the darkness, 'is a man whose spirit is without restraint. Or woman,' I add as an afterthought.

Then I reach one hand up to the top of my pod and run my fingers along the roof until they skim the edges of the rectangular flexi-screen which lies there. Prising it free from the shallow cavity, the small screen begins to glow dully in my hands. Averting my eyes from the words unfurling across the home page, I quickly fold the screen up and slide it beneath my pillow. This is no time to be concerned about the leaderboard.

Before pushing the button and facing whoever is tapping on my pod, I deliberately tense every one of my muscles for a moment and then relax them again, noticing the way the pod moulds gently to the shape of my body. Then I focus all of my attention on the rhythmic whoosh of blood as it rushes through my veins.

Tap, tap, tap. I let the sound fill my senses. The blue glow of my monitor pulses in time with my heartbeat. I can almost feel the soft vibration as *whoever-it-is* taps lightly on the shell of my sanctuary.

I am ready. 'Restraint of feeling, restraint of mind,' I whisper to myself, and then press the circular button nestled in the top of the pod.

I wait, breath held in anticipation. I wonder who – or what – will be waiting for me on the outside.

Nothing happens.

Perhaps I pressed the button too lightly. I try again, jabbing the circle once, twice, half a dozen times with my forefinger. But there is no gentle whoosh of air, no sliver of light from the pod cracking open to reveal the new day. Just darkness. And the tapping, which seems to have grown louder again. *Shit.*

The first seed of doubt takes root in my stomach but I quickly stifle the growing sense of unease. So, I am trapped; no big deal. No pod has ever malfunctioned before – I am sure of it – and it couldn't simply be a coincidence that my own release button had failed to work at the exact moment that a strange tapping sound had begun. This is clearly part of the architects' design. This is a test.

Maybe it's not? There is a small whisper in the back of my mind and I quickly silence the traitorous voice. Of course it is a test. But my body refuses to listen to my rational thoughts, and despite my best efforts I can feel my heart rate quicken and my breathing become shallower. *Far out. Have they given me a broken pod?* The monitor on my wrist glows a brighter blue and then changes to amber as the tapping continues. My pod, which felt like a sanctuary a moment before, now feels like a coffin from the *old world*. Get a grip, Eve.

Maybe it's not a test? says the little voice again. *Unless there's someone - or something - prowling around in the multi, tapping one long claw on the top of your pod.* At that moment, a metallic scraping sound reverberates through the base of my pod, shuddering through my flesh and settling disquietingly in the pit of my stomach.

Clenching my eyes tightly shut, I try to recall all that Professor Quin has taught us in Virtues Education. I can see the ageing Professor in my mind gesturing towards a 3D reconstruction of the human brain.

'The amygdala is the integrative centre for emotions -' I begin aloud, but then another sound joins the tapping and scraping and I falter.

'It's me,' says a familiar voice between painfully loud gasps and I freeze. It can't be him. It isn't possible. 'Evie, come and see what they've done to me.'

My monitor turns the colour of the overseers' jumpsuits — a deep bloody crimson. My eyes sting with hot tears and I feel a new emotion overtake me — one that I have rarely felt before. What is the word for it? I can't recall the term but my body quickly fills with a different desire, and instead of wanting to curl into a ball, I have an overwhelming need to scream at the architects for how unfair this is. How unfair it all is.

I punch the button in the roof of my pod again and am rewarded with a satisfying sting of pain in my knuckles. Nothing happens, no gentle click of the lock disengaging, but I continue to punch the button another three times — just in case. I can only hope that I'm not the only student locked in my pod right now, and that we are all experiencing similar hallucinations; that we are all on a similar playing field. Of course, it's not so even after all, is it? Nobody else will be hearing the voice of their culled brother outside their pod.

That's the thing that has filled my body with this new emotion – *anger*, that's the word I was looking for. Using Luc's voice is a dirty move by the architects, and I am annoyed. No, I am *pissed off!* A little thrill shoots through my body as I recall some more of the banned words. I don't say them aloud and risk an infraction, but with my life spiralling out of control they certainly seem fitting.

Drawing the blanket up to my chin, the little amber lights on my wrist wink out and the darkness once again becomes absolute. But the tapping, scraping and rasping sounds from outside my pod continue. I roll onto my side and hug my knees as best I can in the small space. I try to concentrate on the rhythm of my body and the way my muscles have tensed up as though prepared to run from the ominous being lurking outside. What am I more afraid of - the strange creature with *his* voice or the fact that I have well and truly failed another test?

And then it speaks again.

'Help me, Eve.' The creature coughs, and, despite the thick barrier of the pod around me, I am certain that I hear the splatter of blood or mucus on the floor. I can't ignore it, I have to try the release button again - perhaps it will work now. But as hard as I push, the pod still refuses to open. The creature is whimpering now, a cry of pain or sorrow. 'Evie, you know it's all your fault that I'm gone.'

'It's-not-real-it's-not-real-it's-not-real,' I whisper desperately into the darkness, but my body disagrees.

I clasp my hands over my ears, trying to drown out the painful whimpering, the words, and the cry of anguish that now seems to be coming from *inside* my pod.

The little red flashing lights on my wrist pulse to the beat of my heart.

XXV

If I still entertained any thoughts about recovering from my first redline, the second one quickly crushes them. I don't need to look at the leaderboard to know that I will be scrolling for a good five minutes before I'd be anywhere near finding my name.

My guardians don't speak to me the next morning; perhaps they have already started distancing themselves from me, preparing for another one of their dependants to be culled. It makes sense; after all, why waste time trying to guide a dependant who is too far gone to ever recover.

I start to develop a similar attitude towards the tests. Why bother trying if I'm just going to be culled? I'm tired, and it seems that no matter how hard I try, emotional control is no longer a possibility for me. Birth. Delivery. Dedication. Harvest. Pairing. Transfer. These six milestones of life are not for me. I will only reach four. Birth. Delivery. Dedication. Culled. Just like my brother. I try to tell myself that I'm okay with that.

I'm writing a list in a notebook when Sam slips into the table opposite me at breakfast time. The first thing I notice is the red, raw section of skin on his neck where his stim used to be, and I raise an eyebrow.

'Yeah, stuff that,' he says, and I decide not to ask any more. If he is somehow anointed by the overseers and can get away without a stim, then who am I to judge?

'What are you writing?' he asks.

'A list of emotions.'

'Why?'

'I'm giving up,' I announce, proudly.

'That doesn't sound like you.'

'Oh really, and how long have you known me for? Perhaps I've been giving up for all my life and you just aren't aware of it.'

Of course, my results on the leaderboard belie my words.

'Can you think of any more to add?' I turn the notebook around so that he can read over the list.

He runs a finger down the page, reading over the words, and then looks up at me. 'No,' he says, with some humour in his voice. 'I think you've just about got them all. Are you going to tell me what this is all about?'

I take the notebook back and place a line through the centre of one of the words, splitting it in two. 'I redlined again,' I say. 'Last night.'

Sam nods. 'Understandable. I redlined too, if that's any consolation.'

'It's not.'

Sam laughs. 'Okay, so what's the plan? Back to basics about how to suppress each of those emotions on your list?'

Oh, Sam, you are always so naïve. 'No,' I respond. 'I told you, I'm giving up. If I'm going to be culled anyway, then I may as well see what all the fuss is about.'

He raises an eyebrow. 'What, so you're going to allow yourself to feel?'

'Yes,' I say, decisively. 'For one week, I'm going to feel it all, every single one of these emotions. Sia was right, I've never felt them, not really, so I've never learnt to control them. Distancing myself worked so well for so long…' I shake my head. 'One week,

Sam. No barriers; I'm going to feel them all.'

'Alright,' he says, and I think that he is probably the only person in Eridu who would be supportive of this. 'Which one first?'

I smile at him, and there is a tingling feeling in my stomach.

'That one's happiness,' he says. 'Or maybe excitement.'

I nod. 'Or perhaps I'm terrified, who knows.'

He just laughs again, and I scroll through my timetable on my flexi-screen. I'm rostered on at the transfer centre tonight. Good.

'Fear,' I say at last. 'This afternoon, at the transfer centre, I'm going to let myself feel fear.'

He shakes his head, but he's smiling. 'Okay, then. I don't have any duties tonight so I'll pop in and see how it's going for you. Just try not to get yourself hospitalised again, okay?'

'Thanks.'

I find it easier than I expected to give up my emotional control, to let the walls tumble down and to let the emotions flood my body. Not that there's too many opportunities for strong emotions at the institute, although I allow myself to feel lonely when the other students' eyes glide straight through me. During a mathematics test, I struggle to recall one of the answers but rather than quell the uncomfortable feeling in the pit of my stomach, I embrace it instead. Just for one week, I will experience what it was like to be alive in the *old world*.

I've never felt more prepared to go to the transfer centre. The only thing is, this time it's not because I'm determined not to feel, but the complete opposite.

'We have two transfers this afternoon,' Octavia announces cheerily when I enter the building. Two. This is unprecedented, and I wonder why she would have allowed two families to schedule the transfers on the same day. I feel my heart rate begin to speed up and I make sure that my monitor is concealed beneath my sleeve; I don't want Octavia to send me away before I've really allowed myself to feel fear.

I walk into the back room and sit in a chair in the corner, next to a group of little plants. I look intently at them, aware of the way that they are clinging onto the wall, perfectly in their place, providing the oxygen we all need to survive.

My heart continues to thwack in my chest and I feel prickles of electricity on my back and arms. Is this it, then? Is this fear? I close my eyes and remember walking through the door and seeing the naked shell on the trolley. I recall opening my mouth, about to ask Octavia a question, when the shell sat up, staring blankly at the wall.

I start to feel sick, but I embrace it. The shell in my memories opens its mouth and screams, and screams, and screams. What was it shrieking for? For the essence that had left it? Does it hurt to have your very consciousness ripped out of you?

The feeling consumes me, and my hands start to shake. I am determined to explore the feeling further; what is it really, that makes me feel like this? Was it the screaming shell or something else? Wetness falls into my lap, but it's not red this time. I am crying, but not solely from my eyes. It's like the emotion got caught up in my belly and chest and arms and ricocheted up through my face, spilling out of my eye sockets.

I think I'm scared because I know that one day, probably sooner rather than later, my own essence will be sent to the Grid, and this shell isn't going to want to let go.

I sense, rather than hear someone enter the room.

'I'll be there in a minute,' I say, not even ashamed at the catch in my voice.

A moment later there is pressure on my arm and I stiffen. But it's not Octavia, it's Sam, and I am transported back to Luc helping me up when I fell over, reading me stories, putting his arms around me in the same way that Sam is doing it now. I go to push him off, and then stop. If I've dedicated myself to feeling all of the emotions, then I can't exactly pick and choose now, can I?

'How are you doing?' asks Sam.

'Fine,' I say, and he laughs, because it's obvious that I'm not fine.

The tears continue to stream down my face and this time, when he puts his arms around me, I lean into him.

I can hear his heartbeat through his chest. It is steady and soothing, and he feels both soft and strong at the same time.

If Octavia walked in right now, what would she think? Two people knowing that they are unsuitable for this world gaining comfort from the presence of the other. I imagine I would be banned from the transfer centre. Actually, I'm surprised that I haven't been banned already, just for redlining.

I take a deep breath and pull away, noting the wet patches I've left on Sam's jumpsuit.

'I'm sorry,' I say, but he waves my apology away.

'Everyone has to cry sometimes.'

I shake my head. 'Not in Eridu.'

A bell rings out around the centre and I quickly rub my hands over my face, smearing my tears away.

'How do I look?'

He looks at me, his grey eyes almost translucent.

'Beautiful,' he says at last, and I frown at him. It's inappropriate to say something like that about a person's shell. Although it's true that I have called the foetuses floating in the exo-wombs beautiful before, so I just shrug. Maybe he's trying to make me feel one of the other emotions on my list.

'Thanks.'

My confusion about the double transfer is soon cleared up when I discover that a partnered couple has elected to be transferred at the same time. I can't breathe.

'I can probably do the ceremony for you, if you want,' offers Sam, but I shake my head. I'm going to do this, feelings or not.

I welcome their dependant as warmly as possible, and take her through to a dimly lit room, offering her a seat. Sam follows silently.

'My name is Eve, and this is Sam, we will be here to answer any questions you may have.' Oh Alexa, I can't do this. 'First, the ceremonial drink.'

I pour her a glass of creamy looking liquid and she sips the warm, sweet fluid. Almost instantly, I see her relax, and I half-entertain the thought of pouring myself a cup as well. Of course, that wouldn't be appropriate.

'Have you witnessed a transfer before?'

She shakes her head.

'When you see your guardians, you might get a shock. There will be wires attached to their heads, but it looks more serious than it is.' Am I trying to convince the dependant, or myself?

'You will be asked to repeat a few words, sign some paperwork. And then, when you are ready, Octavia will press a button and your guardians will be transferred to the Grid so they may live on forever.'

'Is it really them?' the dependant asks. 'In the screen?'

I open my mouth to answer, but my throat has gone dry. I can feel my hand start to shake again, so I squeeze it between my legs. She looks at me expectantly.

'It sure is,' says Sam with a broad smile which I'm sure doesn't make her feel any better. It's not natural to smile like that. 'Isn't it amazing what modern science can achieve? We now live in a society where death doesn't exist. Instead, our guardians, our grand-guardians, our dependants can live on forever without fear of overpopulation or depletion of resources. I would call it a miracle, but no; it's science.'

He's probably overdone it, but when Sam offers her another ceremonial drink, she readily accepts, so I doubt she'll remember much anyway.

I refuse to step outside myself, feeling every little emotion as I gaze through the window at the partnered couple, ready to be transferred. The dependant is on one side of me, and Sam is on the other, and we watch in silence as Octavia finishes connecting the wires.

Then, as she prepares to flick the switch, Sam does something I don't expect; he grasps my hand and squeezes tightly. And so we stand there, hearts beating in time, as the hearts encased within the shells on the other side of the window shudder and go still.

XXVI

I half-expect an appointment with the medic to appear on my timetable; after all, I've spent an entire day without attempting to suppress my emotions and the overseers must be aware of it.

However, no appointments are scheduled and I'm able to cross some more emotions off my list. The next day is delivery day, which is one of my favourite ceremonies, so I'm looking forward to experiencing a more enjoyable emotion this time.

Sam sits next to me in the auditorium, and although we hardly speak, I can't stop thinking about the way he held my hand yesterday, and before that, the warm embrace during my meltdown. He's certainly proving useful in helping me experience a range of feelings.

Some milestones slip by quietly with the slitting of an amniotic sac in a darkened room. Others are celebrated in a large lecture hall with all of Eridu present. As we are settled in our seats, overseer Ida takes the centre of the stage and a hush falls over the crowd.

'Welcome,' says the overseer, moving towards the front of the stage, 'to the delivery ceremony.'

Twelve adults walk onto the stage and stand in a line stretched across behind Ida. They have been paired as the overseers see fit, with little ceremony. They are content, of course, with all that will happen. I sit forward in my seat and smile. A few years ago, one of the babies cried and screamed throughout the entire ceremony. I can still remember overseer Nova struggling to power through the ceremony. They sedate the babies now, to avoid such situations. The ceremonies are about reinforcing the values of Eridu, and even the youngest of residents must adhere to the rules. Praise Alexa.

The transition from unborn to born is simple in practice, from watery haven to oxygen-filled world. But it is not one of those events that is paraded in front of everyone. No, birth is one of those quiet connections between baby and foetal monitor, who has been watching and recording them for months. I have witnessed several births during my rounds at the incubation chambers. First, the amniotic tub is removed from its position in the hive-like wall and wheeled through into the adjacent room. This fully formed living being, suspended in liquid, seems quite harmonious before the foetal monitor slices through the outer membrane and reaches in to pull the child into the world. When the child is first removed from the liquid, some of them seem not to notice that they have been born. Others scream and cry instantly. The foetal monitor does a full health check, evaluating whether the child will need additional oxygen or other support, and then the baby is passed on. Not to the guardians, of course; not yet.

'I would like to acknowledge the sacrifice made by our guardians in the past, current guardians, and these future guardians standing here on this stage. And of course, I would like to acknowledge the fathers and mothers of us all; the founders. Praise them.'

'Praise them.'

If I want to experience the full spectrum of emotions this week, I certainly hope that I'm rostered on at the incubation chambers. I look forward to the feeling of wonder permeating my body as I gaze at those floating foetuses.

'Guardianhood is not a duty to be taken lightly,' says Ida. 'These citizens of Eridu have all saved up their oxy-creds and made sacrifices before even being able to apply to become guardians.'

Sacrifices like arranging for your guardians or grand-guardians to be transferred, I think, feeling a little ill.

'The individuals that you see before you have all had their applications approved because of the vigour with which they uphold the six virtues. They have been selectively paired, a strategy from the *old world* to spread the workload when raising children, and they have moved into their new family accommodation in Block A. I am positive you will all make them feel welcome.'

The new guardians stand on the stage, blank-faced, as Ida delivers her speech. I wonder how they feel, about to meet the person that they will be required to care for and nurture over the next seventeen years. But of course, I know how they feel. It's how we should all feel. Content.

'We talk often about the future of Eridu, in light of the reality of our past. We have many ceremonies, but none shows as clear a link to the future as this one right here. These guardians are about to be given perhaps the most important role in all of Eridu; raising the future in the right way. Humanity with purpose.'

'Humanity with purpose,' we reply.

Ida turns slightly, as though she is speaking directly to the guardians, although her voice is loud and clear to us all. 'Eight weeks ago, a number of babies were born in the safety of the birthing rooms. Since then, they have been cared for under the watchful eye of those harvested as nurses.'

I have seen the nurses complete their work, too. For a few weeks, the babies are kept in the nursery under their watchful eyes. They are fed, clothed, toileted and monitored. Always monitored. The period in the nursery is an important one; it is when the children first learn that human connection is not a desired virtue in Eridu. I glance over at Sam, but he is staring straight ahead, watching what is happening on the stage.

The babies are picked up, of course, when they cry. Just not too much, as the rulebook says. And when the babies are finally passed onto their guardians, the rules stand. I think of Tali throwing her arms around me at the preschool. Some children learn the lesson a bit later than others.

'Becoming a guardian is a significant decision. Raising the future of Eridu is an important task, but it does not come without its trials. We all know that wrestling the wild, unrestrained nature of humanity which lies beneath our calm visage can be difficult. But regardless of how difficult this may be, it is nonetheless an important endeavour.'

Ida's speech is different than the ones I have heard Nova deliver. Her manner is the same, and they both speak clearly and engagingly, but I can't say that I have ever heard Nova mention the 'wild, unrestrained nature of humanity' before. For some reason, I think of Sam, sitting beside me. And then I remember my meltdown at the transfer centre yesterday; perhaps I should think of myself.

'Our children have already begun their training in the virtues. Patience, in particular, is the first virtue that they will learn. At first, when the children cry, they will be fed or changed instantly. But as we all know, getting what you want, as soon as you want it — this sense of greed and entitlement is one of the vices that led to the downfall of humanity in the *old world*.'

People nod all around me, and I find myself gazing at the partnered couples standing serenely on the stage. If I am culled, I will never know what it is like to be partnered, or to become a guardian. I try to analyse what I am feeling now. Sadness?

'And so,' continues Ida, 'when the guardians return to their units with the next generation, they will continue to teach them the value of patience by showing them that simply asking for something does not mean that you will get it. In the same way, we too were all taught the virtues. And look around you, at all of those clad in blue. They succeeded in the harvest and have become the future of Eridu. Our hope is that more and more upcoming citizens survive the harvest so that eventually nobody will have to be culled at all.'

Survive is an odd term to use, but I suppose she is referring to the shells. After all, if you don't pass the harvest, then the shell certainly does not survive. Of course, the essence lives on in the Grid.

'These guardians will be supported by both the community and the overseers in a number of ways, and they are encouraged to seek out additional support if they so need it. Raising children is not a solo experience. Already, these babies have been nurtured by the foetal monitors while in the amniotic sacs. They have been fostered by the nurses in the nursery, and now, even though they are being placed in a family unit for the next seventeen years, these guardians are not expected to raise the children alone. They will all begin preschool in just a few weeks, and then the cycle continues. Birth, delivery, dedication, harvest, pairing, and transfer. The six events that mark the stages of life.'

Unless you only get four, I think to myself. Four stages like Luc and the rest of the culled. Possibly four stages for me and Sam too. What happens in the Grid? Do the transferred interact with each other? Will I be content to spend my time hanging out in eternity with Luc? Or is it not that simple.

'These guardians will be on reduced duties while they first settle into their new routine. This is to allow them to spend as much time as possible investing in the future of Eridu. They are encouraged to view all incidents as a teaching experience, and we fully trust that they will raise children who succeed in the harvest in seventeen years.'

I sneak a glance at my own guardians, but they are far too well trained to show anything on their faces. Is it disappointing, I wonder? Do they feel like they have failed Eridu? Or are they told that it's not their fault that Luc was culled. That they did their best.

A moment later, three nurses walk out holding a basket in each hand. Each guardian pair receives a basket and I see them peer in at the contents.

'As you are aware, the overseers are constantly seeking out ways to improve the success rate of the harvest. We work closely with the architects to ensure that the testing is frequent and prepares students in the best way possible. However, it is not always enough.'

This is different. I hear a rustle as people move slightly in their seats. It's all they can do to express their surprise. The guardians on the stage seem too distracted by their new responsibilities to react in any obvious way.

'However, there are still those who do not take the harvest seriously, who treat it all as a game. I'm sure that all of you at the institute will be able to think of at least one person who is still not able to receive one hundred percent on the tests, or to regularly control their emotions. And, worse than that, they seem not to mind.'

I think of Hana. And Tali. I think of myself, and of Sam. Is this directed at us?

'For many of these… idle people, they view the harvest in

abstract terms. It is something that will happen, eventually. But it is of no consequence in the here and now. They are wrong; the harvest is serious, and should be at the forefront of every ranked and unranked student's mind.'

I look around at the grey and brown uniforms.

'Change is inevitable. It is through change that we implement improvement. When the founders first created Eridu, there was no testing, no monitors. It was only through trial and error that the founders worked out the importance of regularly testing students to prepare them for the harvest. And the monitors weren't even a founder invention, they came later in the third or fourth generation. Change is important, if we wish to elicit progress.'

I look around me, but everyone is staring straight ahead.

'New data has been brought to light to show that human connection, as much as it is frowned upon, is still the most likely cause of our harvest rates plateauing. And so, to reduce the likelihood of this avoidable connection ruining our future harvest success rates, there will be changes implemented, starting from the next cycle. Rather than remaining with the same guardians for seventeen years, as has been common practice, children will rotate through guardians. I believe this will give more importance to those two days of the harvest for everyone else, as well as those in their final year. Praise the founders.'

'Praise the founders,' we repeat.

Am I imagining it, or are our voices a little quieter than usual.

The founders created life on the third day, and they numbered the children one, two, three and four. These children became guardians of the others that followed them, and they increased in number.

Book of Eridu

XXVII

A change in guardians, every single cycle. It seems unthinkable, and yet if that's what is holding our harvest scores down, then of course it makes sense. I'm sure that we all want to do whatever it takes to increase the pass rate so that fewer people are culled. Part of me is thankful that this is my final cycle, as at least the changes aren't going to affect me. Yet. One day, if I pass the harvest and am partnered and go through the delivery ceremony, I will know that the child I am to become the guardian of will only be in my presence for a single cycle, and then it will change.

I think of the love sickness that Ida was telling me about. Who am I to judge?

It's day two of *operation: feel emotions*, but other than experiencing slight surprise during the delivery ceremony, I haven't managed to cross any more emotions off my list. Thankfully, there are some areas of Eridu that I know are more likely to make me feel than others.

I decide to take the long way home, and Sam follows me, although I'm not sure what I think about that. As I step inside the tunnel, it feels slightly cooler than out, but it's just an illusion because it's darker in here than out in the courtyard. Being underground, every part of Eridu is a comfortable 22 degrees.

We walk in silence, listening to the gentle thud as our feet hit the ground. The rock curves down toward us, but the hands seem almost welcoming this afternoon.

'I haven't seen a tunnel like this before,' says Sam, breaking the silence. 'It looks old.'

'You don't say.'

He smiles good-naturedly and jogs a little to catch up with me.

'That was an interesting ceremony.'

'Yes,' I say, as we reach the fence looking out over the large space and the secret door. I stop, leaning against the fence, and Sam joins me.

'So, do you really believe in all that stuff that Ida was saying?' Sam asks.

'What stuff?'

'You know, about human connection being bad.'

'Of course,' I say, and I can't quite make out the expression on his face. Is he thinking about when we held hands in the transfer centre, too? But of course, it's just for a week, just so I can feel them all once before clamping down on the emotions properly.

'But why?' he says.

'Sam, you probably know the Book of Eridu better than I do by now.'

'I want to hear it in your own words. Why do you need to suppress emotions?'

'Because of the war, and the darkness - '

'Yeah, okay, so anger and greed are probably good ones to eliminate, and I can see why the founders wanted a society devoid of jealousy. But what about happiness?'

'Oh, Sam,' I say, allowing myself to laugh. It sounds a little unnatural, and echoes around the space. 'You've misunderstood. Everyone is allowed to feel happy.'

'No, you are allowed to feel content. True happiness doesn't feel like floating in a calm lake. It feels like swimming in the sea, diving beneath the waves and being carried from one feeling of elation to another.'

'What, you've swum in a lake or the sea before, have you?' I ask, teasing.

He smiles, and then reaches one hand out as though to touch my hand, but quickly changes his mind and his arm drops to his side. I'm not sure if I'm glad or disappointed.

I find it hard to believe that he is working for the overseers, and yet… Silence spreads between us, but it is not the awkward stillness that you want to escape from quickly. No, this silence is surprisingly companionable. I gaze out at the door across the chamber and consider pointing it out to him, but I change my mind. It's something special between me and Luc.

'It's called love.'

I look at him, eyebrows raised.

'What you feel when you think about Luc. The thing that you keep trying to ignore.'

'I know what love is,' I snap, my monitor going amber.

'It's okay, it's one of the good emotions.'

'There are no good emotions.'

'Sure there are. If you don't have love then you aren't really living.'

I laugh again, but it feels cold rather than filled with humour. It echoes strangely around the tunnel and the empty space beyond the fence. I can't be bothered arguing with him.

'It's nice to see you relaxing, feeling for once. I suppose that's the freedom you get from being last on the leaderboard.'

'Second-to-last,' I correct him.

He smiles. 'Right.'

The reason I am allowing myself to feel has little to do with thinking that it is acceptable, and everything to do with finally giving up.

'I think I'm ready to tell you the truth,' he says quietly. 'If you still want to hear it?'

I nod, feeling that emotion again – curiosity – blossom within me.

'Okay, Eve. Here goes.' He stares out across the empty space and I get the feeling that he doesn't want to meet my eyes. His monitor goes amber. 'Eve, I'm not from here. Not really.'

This is new. I thought he was going to admit that he was working for the overseers, or that perhaps he didn't have to obey the same rules as everyone else because he was the dependant of one.

'Where are you from then?' I ask. 'The surface?' I think of the vision of deformed humans slowly dying of radiation poisoning and viruses, but the image doesn't seem to fit with the young man standing in front of me.

Sam places one hand on the wire fence and leans against it, still refusing to look at me. 'I'm from the Grid.' His voice is strained and quiet.

I just shake my head. 'What?'

'They finally worked out how to do it, Eve. How to bring people back.'

I shake my head, remembering the screaming shell. 'No.'

'It's true.' He still won't look at me, and I try to put two and two together.

I run my eyes down his body, realisation landing in my stomach with a sickening plop.

'So if you're really from the Grid, then your shell…?'

He sighs, running a hand through his hair. It sticks up slightly and I suppress the urge to set it straight.

'Yeah, this shell isn't exactly the one I was in before. This is a newly vacated one.'

My skin crawls. When he says it, all the little parts of the puzzle click into place and a strange, warm feeling courses through my body.

'Oh.' I think of all the things I said about transfers and the Grid. All of my criticism, wondering if the visions encased in my screen were really the consciences of people who had been prised out of their shells. And here is one, standing in front of me.

'So the screaming shell I saw at the transfer centre?'

'I guess your guardians were right. It was just the body struggling to let go.'

I guess so. So the people in the screen are real after all, not copies. My heart hammers in my chest, and my hands shake slightly. This is a new emotion, one that I am certain I have never felt before. Sam turns and looks at me.

'Revulsion,' he suggests.

I shake my head. 'Sam, you don't understand. This is the best news I could ever have received.'

Sam smiles at me, but it seems a little sad. I'm not sure why.

'I have to go. I have to tell Luc.'

He nods, and then turns away again, looking out through the fence. I wonder if he has noticed the little door.

I hesitate for a moment. 'Sam, are you coming back to Block A?'

'Not right now.' His voice sounds vacant, as though he is speaking from far away. 'You go and talk to your brother, I'll see you later on.'

I don't need to be told twice. I jog through the tunnels, knowing that I should care more about my emotional control. After all, if Sam was able to come back from the Grid, then Luc might be able to as well. He could try the harvest again, and this time he could succeed. And I want to be there right alongside him.

*All emotions are unhelpful, but some are more dire than others. And of all
those emotions that we seek to remove, love is the most dangerous of all.*

Book of Eridu

XXVIII

I plan out what I'm going to say before I activate the program. I
haven't spoken to Luc at all through the transfer system, and I'm
not sure how he's going to react. If I was culled, and then my own
sibling refused to speak to me, how would I feel? But he must
remember my anxiety about the transfer centre. Surely he will
forgive me.

I open up my notebook and jot down a few ideas, and then
activate the transfer program. It's strange, after being used to
seeing someone every single day, to suddenly transition to not
seeing them at all. And now, as my finger hovers above the button
that will allow me to speak to Luc, I find myself struggling to press
it.

I look around myself. It's difficult, now that I'm in the multi,
to find anywhere private, so I'm out in the courtyard, sitting on a
bench under a birch tree. I close my eyes, imagining the world in
the story books that Luc used to read me. Maybe I would feel the
soft caress of the wind, and hear the rustle of the leaves. Maybe
there would be birds chirping and bees buzzing around me,
fertilising the plants. Nowadays, it is all done by people.

I swallow, and then push the button, and Luc's face appears a
moment later encased in the screen.

'Hey, Evie.'

I can't speak. I just stare at him, noticing the way his dark hair
is cropped short, exactly as it was before he was culled. I let the
excitement, or hope, or whatever it is course through my veins. I

can even ignore the glint in his eyes.

'Hey, Luc,' I say, smiling. It feels nice, letting the smile stem from the inside. 'How's it going in the Grid?'

He smiles far more easily than he did in Eridu. 'It's great, Eve. Moving to the Grid is the best thing I ever did.'

I don't remind him that it wasn't his choice, that he failed the harvest and was sent there against his will. It seems unimportant right now.

'That's great, Luc. Look… I wanted to talk to you about something.' *Thump, thump, thump* goes my heart.

'Is it about the harvest? Eve, you will be fine, just keep working on that emotional control.'

I don't tell him about my current leaderboard ranking. 'Actually, it's not about me. It's about you.'

He stares out of the screen at me, and I look down at the notes scrawled onto paper in the old fashioned way.

'I've recently become aware,' there is a catch in my voice, and I feel like crying even though I am happy. How strange. I clear my throat. 'I've become aware of a way that you could return to Eridu.'

I hold my breath, waiting for his response. I thought he would look surprised, at least, but instead he just continues to stare at me. Maybe the transfers already know and it is not surprising news to him at all. Perhaps when you transfer you are privy to all of the knowledge in Eridu, accessible with a single thought.

'I met someone who used to be in the Grid,' I continue. 'The overseers implanted his consciousness into another shell, and he's back here, walking and talking in Eridu.'

Luc smiles at me. 'Oh, that's great, Eve. I was worried that you might not cope well with me being culled. I'm happy that you have found some other people to hang around with.'

'No, Luc -' I frown at him. 'That's not the bit that I wanted you to focus on. Didn't you hear me? He used to be in the Grid, now he's back in Eridu.'

Luc nods. 'Wonderful, praise progress.'

'Luc, don't you see?' I lower my voice as another student exits Block A and walks past me on his way to the tunnels. 'Maybe you could come back too. I'm not sure how they select the candidates, but perhaps you could ask to be...' I search for the word... 'Untransferred.'

Luc smiles at me, and I ignore the gleam in his eyes; it's just the updated graphics card. The fact that Sam came from the Grid is proof that my scepticism was unfounded.

'Eve, being in the Grid is different than Eridu, but it isn't bad. I like being here.'

'What, so are you saying you don't want to come back? To be with me?'

My monitor is already amber, but when I imagine that my own brother doesn't want to leap at the chance of returning to Eridu, it threatens to go crimson.

'Eve,' his voice is softer now, the way it used to be when I was little and he would explain something new that he had learnt. 'That's exactly what I'm saying. I don't want to come back to Eridu, and I'm sure all of the transfers would say the same thing.'

Thump, thump, thump. The excitement, the hope, implodes inwards. I shut the program off without saying goodbye.

XXIX

I walk along the corridor of pale doors, looking for number 32. When I find it, I hesitate for a moment before knocking. What if his guardians answer? I realise that I don't even know who Sam's guardians are.

I raise my fist to knock, and then let my hand drop to my side again. I replay my conversation with Luc – or the imprint of Luc – in my mind. *I don't want to come back to Eridu*, that's what he said.

Before I can change my mind, I rap sharply on the door, three quick knocks. Perhaps he's not here. Perhaps Sam was lying about being in a unit, and his pod is really in some obscure corner of the multi where the low-ranked ought to be.

But there's a sound on the other side of the door, and a moment later there he is, standing on the threshold.

As soon as I see him, I can't talk.

'Eve, what's wrong?'

I press my lips together tightly and shake my head. Sam looks up and down the corridor before ushering me inside, closing the door behind him. His guardians' pods are closed, and Sam sees my glance.

'There's nobody in them. I wasn't assigned guardians when I came here. One of the architects just checks up on me now and then.'

I nod, not even trying to sort this revelation out in my mind, and Sam gestures towards the seat tucked under his desk. I just shake my head again; I'm too agitated to sit down. I cross my arms across my chest as though that will somehow help me to contain all of my emotions.

'It wasn't him,' I say, my voice tight with emotion.

'What? Come sit down.'

I shake my head again. 'It wasn't Luc. I was right all along, they don't really transfer your essence, they just copy it, and when they copied Luc, well they mucked it up.'

'Eve, what are you talking about?'

I desperately need for the person in the screen not to be my brother. Because my brother wouldn't betray me like that, he wouldn't refuse to come back and be with me. I think that's what I always hated about the transfer system, because I wasn't sure if the shell was screaming because it didn't want to give up, or because the essence had never left.

But what is that saying about Sam? And where is the real Luc if the transfer isn't him? I don't want to think about it.

'Sam, what's so good about the Grid?' My voice sounds like it's coming from some place far away.

Sam doesn't answer straight away. He sits in the base of his pod and gazes across at me, as though working out what to say.

'I don't know. It's *different* than here.'

'Do you want to go back to the Grid?'

He shrugs. 'Yes and no. Why are you asking?'

I can't stand still anymore. I walk over to Sam's desk and look at the various books on his shelf so that I don't have to look at his grey eyes. Most people don't have a lot of books – he must have borrowed them from the library too. 'I spoke to Luc. He says he doesn't want to come back.' There's a catch in my voice, but Sam ignores it.

'Maybe because he's finally allowed to feel.'

Is that it, then? Is it really as simple as that? 'What's so good about feeling? I've gone my entire life without feeling anything. I was content. And then over the past few days I've felt grief, fear, and anger. Trust me, there is nothing good about feeling those emotions.'

My monitor is already streaked with red and I take a deep breath. Whatever I'm feeling right now isn't exactly enjoyable.

'Eve, come sit down.'

I turn around and Sam pats the space beside him in the pod base. I hesitate for a moment and then walk over and sit down, hoping he can give me some insight into my brother's complete refusal to entertain the idea of returning to Eridu.

'It's not him, is it?'

Sam doesn't look at me as he talks, but he does shift slightly so that his right arm presses lightly against my left.

'I don't know, Eve. You probably know a lot more about the transfer centre than I do. And in terms of emotions, well you're right, in a way. Grief, anger, fear… Those are three emotions that aren't at all enjoyable. There's other ones too, though, that aren't so bad.'

'Sam, when Luc told me that he didn't want to come back to Eridu, it felt like someone physically reaching inside my chest cavity and ripping out my heart.'

Sam puts his arm around me and I don't pull away. I just feel so tired.

'That's because you love him,' he says softly.

He must be right.

'I guess I'd better cross that one off my list.'

For some reason, I actually quite like this shell and the idea of leaving it sends little prickles down my arms.

'Have you ever felt love?'

I feel him nod.

'It sucks, doesn't it?'

His laugh reverberates through his body and into my own. 'Not at all. Love is one of those good emotions.'

'No way,' I say, pulling away from him slightly so that I can see the expression on his face. I think he is being serious. 'Wars have been fought in the name of love.'

'I know, but that doesn't mean that the emotion itself is bad.'

'Sure it does, if nobody feels love. If nobody feels anything, then we can't make the mistakes we made before.'

'At least you are saying we, now, instead of they.'

I contemplate this for a moment. 'So who did you love?'

'It's not past tense. I did – do – love my parents.'

'You mean the founders? Or are you talking about your guardians.'

'Back in my day,' says Sam, 'guardians were called parents.'

'Were they in the Grid with you?'

He shakes his head again.

'I'm sorry. I guess they were a bit less strict on emotions back when you were transferred, hey?'

'I guess so.'

'Tell me about your life.'

'In the Grid?'

I shake my head. 'No, before the Grid.'

He is quiet for a while, and I become aware of the way his arm is draped loosely around my body.

'It was a long time ago and I hardly remember it.'

'Don't give me that.'

'What?'

'That's what the transfers always say when I ask them about the harvest.' I wonder if he is offended by me calling them transfers; it seems too impersonal now that I know someone from the Grid. But is it really him, though? The original Sam? Or is he just a copy of the original. Maybe it doesn't matter.

He shrugs. 'I suppose it's strange being in the Grid, you lose touch with your previous life.'

'And how did they bring you back?'

'I'm not sure of the specifics, but basically, the scientists figured that if they could do it one way, then they could reverse the procedure.'

'So, when did you transfer?'

'A long time ago.'

Of course it was a long time ago. A time when there were parents and sicknesses. And love.

'So you're like… really old?'

'I suppose.'

I try to put it together, to make it make sense, but I'm struggling.

'But why?'

He gazes out across the room as though the answers lie on his bookshelf. 'To see if they could.'

His monitor is amber, and I realise something else.

'Sam, they shouldn't have sent you into the final cycle. You are never going to pass the harvest.'

'They never intended me to pass the harvest.'

I go cold.

'So you get to stay in Eridu, even if you don't pass?'

He doesn't look at me, or answer me, and I realise the awful truth. 'Oh, Sam.'

'It's alright. I had a job to do, I came for a while, I got to eat good food, and feel warm, and safe.'

'You don't feel safe in the Grid?'

He doesn't answer me. 'And then I will leave. At least I got to meet you.'

We've been sitting there, together, for so long but I never really paid attention to how close we were. When I look up at him I realise that if I'm going to experience the full spectrum of emotions, there's one more that I want to try.

He doesn't push me away as I lean forward and press my lips against his. They are warm and soft and taste almost sweet.

A moment later I realise what I've done, and I quickly stand up. Both of our monitors are crimson now.

'I have to go.'

'Goodbye, Eve.' For some reason, he sounds sad.

XXX

On the third day of my *week of feeling*, I get to cross off another emotion; embarrassment. Sam doesn't bring up the previous day, and neither do I, but the kiss stretches out between us, making our interactions more awkward than usual.

Thankfully, when I check my timetable, I have something to break the silence with.

'I'm rostered on at the incubation chambers tonight. Do you still want to come?'

Sam checks his own schedule. 'Sure,' he replies, and I smile at him, feeling warm. It helps to make up for the coldness I feel whenever another student stares straight through me.

My days at the institute are bearable – just – but being treated like I'm invisible is certainly a new experience. I hope that once the week is up, I will find some new resolve to suppress the emotions and begin crawling back up the leaderboard. And then what will happen to my friendship with Sam?

I don't want to think about that.

That afternoon, the incubation chambers are dark and hushed as usual. When I turn the lights on, the exo-wombs encased in the hive glow with an ethereal blue-green light.

'Woah,' says Sam. 'Intense. Are they really...'

'Foetuses? Yes.'

He walks around the side of the tanks and peers into the murky liquid, entranced. 'Why don't you just have babies the natural way?'

I suppress a shudder. There is nothing natural about… that. 'Because we are all the sons and daughters of the founders.'

Sam laughs, but doesn't look at me, seemingly unable to take his eyes off the closest foetus suspended in the liquid. On the sides of the tanks are screens monitoring oxygen levels, nutrient delivery, and a range of other factors.

'Something to do with the feelings thing, yeah?' he asks. 'You figure you have to create life artificially for fear of the parents forming a bond or something? That's so stuffed up.'

'*We*, Sam. You are as much a part of this as all of us.'

But he's not, is he. He would have been created in the same way as all of us, and yet as a low-ranked student he is naïve about the entire process. I do wonder why, out of all of the essences in the Grid, they would bring back someone so emotionally unstable. They could have brought back Luc instead, although I'm not sure how I'd feel about seeing Luc in a new body.

Or maybe Sam *was* high ranked in his own time, I think. Perhaps he just forgot how to control his emotions during his time in the Grid. But even if he somehow manages to pass the harvest – which is virtually impossible – he will never be destined to work in a position at the incubation chambers. He'll be a food server, or a cleaner, earning the lowest number of oxy-creds possible. He probably won't ever be able to bank up enough to apply to be partnered and to become a guardian.

I probably shouldn't be showing him this. Even being rostered on at the transfer centre was overstepping his rank. I wonder again why the overseers did it.

How much should I tell him? How much would he want to know?

'It's not so much about the emotional bond this time, Sam.'

He turns away from the tanks, clearly curious. 'What is it then?'

I hesitate and then lead him over to a large freezer in the corner.

'In here,' I say slowly, wondering if I'm going to regret this. 'Frozen since those early cycles, is the genetic material of the founders.'

Sam stares at the fridge with some un-diagnosable expression. 'What, have you got their bodies stored in there or something?'

I sigh, sliding open a little panel on the door of the freezer so that he can see inside the glass. 'Not bodies.' He peers in, staring at the rows of containers, and then looks back at me in confusion. He doesn't get it. Of course he doesn't get it. I should just shut up now.

'Eggs,' I say at last, closing the little panel. 'And sperm.'

'What?' His eyebrows shoot up into his hairline.

'We are the sons and daughters of the founders.'

He rubs a hand through his hair and glances back at the freezer as though the genetic material might suddenly jump out and accost him. I can't see his monitor under the sleeve of his jumpsuit, but I can imagine what it shows.

'I didn't think you meant literally.'

He walks away from the freezer and back to the exo-wombs, peering once again into the liquid. Perhaps he's looking for tell-tale signs of what I have just told him. Similar facial features; the same cheekbones or snub nose.

'But why?'

'There were only six founders, Sam,' I say, walking over to join him. 'The rest of humanity was wiped out, or close to it. They had to do what they could to save the human race.'

He is silent, and we listen to the gentle beeping sounds of the tanks. 'If the founders had elected to have children naturally they would have ended up with how many children. Eight? Even if each couple produced ten or twelve children, it wouldn't save us. Not to mention that there wouldn't be enough genetic diversity once you got to the third or fourth generation. So they stockpiled sperm and eggs, enough to last us, at least until we found more survivors or came up with another solution.' I place one hand on the side of the amniotic tank, gazing through at the perfectly formed foetus encased within. 'Of course, it looks like they were the only immune survivors, nobody else has come forward. So we will stay here until the radiation settles, the darkness clears, and the virus runs its course, so we can eventually return to the surface.'

'But that's not sustainable.' His voice sounds strained.

'Sure it is,' I reply. 'And when we get close to running out, it's simple enough to extract material from any of the sons or daughters of the founders.'

'Like you.'

'And you.' He makes a face.

'So you're all like… brothers and sisters.'

'We,' I correct him, again. 'And not exactly. There were six founders – three women and three men. Some of us are full brothers and sisters, some half, and some not genetically related at all.'

I look at Sam now, and wonder which combination he was created from. I'm not even sure who my own genetic parents are; we find that out after the harvest. Over the years, with my emotional control, I have been certain that I'm a daughter of Alexa, but these days I'm not so sure. As to my father, who knows.

'So your guardians could technically be your older siblings.'

'Yes, I suppose.'

He walks along the tanks to the side where the foetuses are

smaller, less developed. I can't make out the expression on his face.

'Do they all survive?'

'Once they reach this stage, generally, yes. But in the earlier stages there are a few casualties. Follow me.'

I lead him through to the next room where the youngest foetuses are being analysed by Bes.

'Hi, Eve.'

'Hey, Bes. Successful day?'

Bes nods at me distractedly. 'Very. Ten eggs were fertilised yesterday, so far seven are progressing nicely.'

Sam walks over towards the trays with open fascination, and Bes looks at him without saying anything.

'I've only just started working out how to do this,' I admit. 'But basically, once they have reached five days old, they are implanted in these biosacs here and numbered.' I point to the clear sacs being oxygenated through large machines.

'Then, they are transplanted into the larger amniotic tubs, the exo-wombs you saw on the way in.'

'Tahi, rua, toru, wha,' reads Sam off the small biosacs. What is this?'

'Names,' explains Bes. 'With the founders, it was all numbers, but once the population increased, we needed a better system of naming, so we name them after numbers in different languages. A bit more personal, you see, while still embracing the views of the founders.'

'Personal?'

I glance sharply at Sam. I shouldn't even have brought him in here, and if he makes a scene then it isn't only going to be him who gets into trouble. 'This is what I wanted to show you,' I say to him, gesturing towards the numbers on the side of the bio-sacs.

'It looks similar to what we saw in the Book of Eridu, right?'

Sam nods. 'So they are named after numbers, and then the parents – I mean guardians – choose a new name?'

'No, the names stick,' says Bes. 'My name is Bes, which is five in Turkish.'

'No way.' He turns to me. 'Eve, you aren't named after a number.'

'Yes, I am. You will be as well. We all are. Mine is from the Ayiwoo language, if I remember correctly. I only know that because I've worked here so often. Most students are unaware of the meaning of their names.'

'That's right,' says Bes. 'Eve is number three in Ayiwoo, and when Eve was in the exo-wombs, she would have been the third one along on the row.'

'No way,' says Sam again, running one hand through his pale hair.

'It's true,' I say to Sam, smiling in what I hope is a reassuring way. 'Lil, or Lilu, means two. And you know Polee, don't you? Her name means eight in the same language.'

'And you're okay with this?' says Sam, and his voice is louder than acceptable. Bes is staring at him, and I realise that I need to get him out of here before he makes a scene.

'Why wouldn't I be? Come on, it's time for you to leave.'

'This,' he shakes his head, gesturing at everything in the room. 'This was not in the Book of Eridu.'

'Sure it was.' I think for a moment, trying to recall the exact wording. 'The founders created life on the third day, and they numbered the children one, two, three and four. These children became guardians of the others that followed them, and they increased in number.'

'That doesn't mean that they literally called them by numbers.'

'Sam…'

I catch a glimpse of his monitor, and it is already amber, tinged with streaks of crimson. It looks like blood.

'I should have known you wouldn't be able to handle it.'

He shakes his head.

'I had parents, Eve. Parents who I loved - '

'Love is a dangerous emotion,' I begin automatically.

'No it's not, goddammit.' His voice is louder now, and Bes stares at him. I can work out what she is thinking.

'I have to get out of here,' he says at last, and I nod encouragingly. Then he turns on his heel and marches out the door.

I suppose that's why the low-ranked aren't usually shown the more important places in Eridu. They just can't handle the truth.

XXXI

Sam isn't at breakfast the following morning, and I replay yesterday in my mind a hundred times, wishing I had never taken him to the incubation chambers. What an idiot. I should head to the institute, and to my classes, but I need to see if he's okay.

I hadn't really understood how attached he was to the concept of parents and love until his outburst. I suppose I should have foreseen it, with all his talk of guardians being called parents and love not being a sickness. We clearly come from different worlds.

But what was up with his reaction to the incubation chambers? It's one of my favourite places in Eridu, and yet the whole concept had clearly made his skin crawl. I suppose it's similar to my feelings about the transfer centre; I don't understand it, but that doesn't really matter, does it? All that matters is that he freaked out and it was my fault. I've never seen someone get angry like that, and it could have been avoided. I can't deny the fact that he's probably going to be culled anyway, but it's not a nice feeling knowing that you are responsible for someone redlining.

I walk down the corridor towards Sam's unit. The hallways are deserted because everyone else has already gone down to breakfast. 30, 31, 32. He might not even be there; perhaps he skipped breakfast and went straight to the institute. As I reach out to knock on his door, I hear a strained voice emanating from within.

Instead of knocking, I wait, listening. There is a muffled male

193

voice, and then I hear Sam speaking, louder this time.

'Just for a few more days.'

There's another inaudible reply, and then I hear footsteps coming across the unit and towards the door. I step back into the corridor, but there is nowhere to conceal myself so I just stand there as a tall man dressed in crimson opens the door and steps out into the corridor.

I gape at him, but although I am standing right there in front of him, he walks past me without so much as a glance. Of course, those in the premium positions rarely interact with everyone else. Architect or overseer? Architect, definitely. But why here, talking to Sam? I remember what Sam said, about having no guardians, but that an architect checked up on him. That must be the explanation for it, but it's a strange arrangement, isn't it? Even if he is a returned transfer.

I knock lightly on the door, but there is no response. Turning the handle, I discover that the door is unlocked and I step over the threshold.

Sam is sitting in the base of his pod, staring at the floor, but he looks up when I enter the room. He seems tired, his face strained, but the edges of his lips lift momentarily in a half-hearted attempt to greet me.

'Sam, what's going on?'

Sam pats one hand on the pod next to him, and I hesitate. 'I'm sorry about yesterday, it was dumb. I didn't mean to freak you out.'

He just shakes his head and smiles, but his smile looks sad, and I cross the room and sit in the base. He takes my hand in his and we sit there in silence.

'Sam?'

He traces one finger over my monitor which is transitioning

between blue and amber, blue and amber.

'Sam, what's going on?'

'We're friends, aren't we?'

'Yes,' I say, wondering where he is going with this.

'And you have felt… something over the past few days?'

Is he referring to what I feel for him, or just that I've experienced emotions in general? I squeeze his hand. 'You know I have.'

He nods, then rubs one hand over his face.

'Sam, what's wrong?'

He lets go of my hand and stands, walking across to the other side of the room. The other pods are hanging against the wall, closed but vacant, and he leans against one now.

'Architect Nik just came to inform me that I'm leaving.'

I go cold.

'Leaving where?'

He doesn't answer me.

'Back to the Grid?' I suggest, but I don't really want to know the answer after all.

Sam hesitates for a long moment before replying. 'Yes.'

'Already? But Sam, why? Why not let you get through to the harvest.' There's a catch in my voice that won't go away.

'Why do you think?'

I imagine the leaderboard, with Sam's name, unmoving, right at the bottom.

'But, Sam, they set you up for failure. Bringing you into the final cycle like that. There was never any real possibility…'

He nods. 'Just a little experiment, Eve. Just to see if they could do it. If they could bring someone back.' His eyes are red, but he isn't crying. I wonder what it's like to have your essence jammed into a new shell like that.

'When do you leave?' My heart is thudding in my chest.

'Tonight.'

'No.'

Sam does smile, now, but sadly. Is it possible to combine two contrasting emotions like that? I suppose the proof is in front of me.

'Well, the architect has only just left. If you walk quickly, you might be able to catch up with him and tell him what you think.'

When I look at Sam, I can see the wires that will soon be sprouting out of his temples. He already has his foot halfway into the other world, just like me.

'But you can't just do that. You can't come into someone's life and disrupt it in that way, only to leave again.' I'd like to pretend that my voice was even and my monitor pale, but that would be a lie.

'Eve…' says Sam, walking back over to the pod. He tries to take my hand, but I pull it away. I'm going to have to get used to being alone again pretty soon, I may as well start now.

'Eve, it's not exactly my choice. I'd stay if I could.'

'But how long for? Until the harvest? And then it's all over, isn't it. You go back to the Grid and I stay here, if I'm lucky. It's probably better that you leave now. Get it over with.'

The words taste bitter in my mouth, and as soon as I say them, I want to take them back. Sam just nods, however, seemingly unphased. First Luc, now Sam. I can see why anything more serious than a superficial friendship is forbidden in Eridu.

And then I make up my mind, pushing my fears aside for now. After all, I know that there's a way to be reunited with Luc and to stay with Sam.

'I'll fail the harvest.'

At first, Sam doesn't understand my tone of voice. 'Have some confidence, Eve, if you focus, you can get back up there.'

'No, I mean deliberately,' I say, and the more I think about it, the more it seems like an excellent plan.

'Well that's a foolish idea,' says Sam.

'Is it? But it would mean that I could be with you, and with Luc.'

'I thought you didn't believe in the transfers. I thought you said they were imperfect copies of reality, or something like that.'

I shrug. Maybe Sam is just a copy of the previous Sam, and his original identity was destroyed when his body was turned into fertiliser. But what is the difference between a copy and its original, if it is close enough that nobody recognises the difference?

But if it's a copy, where does my true essence go?

'Tell me, Sam, what's it like in the Grid?'

He just shrugs.

'Does time stretch out before you indefinitely? Do you float, suspended in an alternate state of being like the foetuses in the exo-wombs?' I ask hopefully.

'Sure.'

'And you can feel, right? You can feel whatever and whenever you like?'

'Eve - '

'Right?'

'Eve, listen to me. You don't want to go to the Grid unless it's absolutely necessary. You are better off here.'

There is a moment of silence, and I feel my heart beating fiercely in my chest.

'What, you don't want me to be there with you, is that it? If time really does stretch out indefinitely then you don't want to spend that time with me?'

'Eve-'

'No, Sam,' I say, my monitor a bright amber. 'I've made up my mind, I'll fail the harvest. Hell, maybe I should just come with you tonight to the transfer centre and ask them to transfer me at the same time.'

Sam sighs, rubbing his hand through his hair again so that it spikes up. 'Eve, I need to tell you something.'

The way he says it stops me mid-rant. What else could he possibly tell me to trump his news that he is leaving?

'Eve,' he says, slowly. 'I wasn't solely brought to Eridu as an experiment to see if it was possible. I also had a purpose. A job, set out for me by one particular architect.'

'Architect Nik?'

'Right.'

'Okay?'

He rubs his hand over his face as though working out what to say.

'Eve, if I tell you this, you need to promise me that you will try in the harvest. That in the weeks leading up to it you will suppress those emotions and study hard.'

'But you're the one who told me to feel things. I don't understand...'

'Eve, promise me.'

'No. Tell me what the architect asked you to do and then I'll make up my mind.'

He tries to take my hand again but I pull it away.

'Okay, here goes.' He looks directly at me as he speaks, and I resist the urge to look away from the intense gaze. 'He told me that there was this girl at the top of the leaderboard. She was so good, that he doubted that she'd ever felt... anything.'

My heart thuds in my chest. 'Let me guess, her name was Eve.'

'Right. He said to me that I could come to Eridu, at least for a while, if I did one thing.'

'Which was?' But I already know what he is going to say.

'He wanted me to make you feel.'

I feel it all right now, I am flooded with feelings. They are all that I am; no shell, just emotions.

'He wanted you to make me feel what, exactly?' My voice comes out more stable than I expected.

'Anything. Everything. He told me to talk to you about Luc, about the transfer centre.'

'And he told you to make me fall in love with you.'

His eyebrows shoot up. 'Eve, this thing that we have going here. I'm not sure that you'd exactly describe it as love.'

Clearly not. I breathe deeply, building up the internal walls but they keep crumbling. My voice is perfectly even. 'Why did the architect want me to feel emotions? What was the purpose?'

'I'm not sure, Eve. Maybe he just wanted to do it for kicks, to see if somebody so immune to emotion could be persuaded to feel. Maybe he secretly wants you to fail in the harvest. Perhaps the architects have some sort of betting process going on, and he knows that if he can get you to fail then he will win the sweepstakes. Eve, he didn't tell me why, he just told me what to do.'

I'm still trying to catch up. 'So let me get this straight. The overseers decide to send your consciousness back into a body, just to see if it can be done. But once you're here, an architect points to me and says, *see that girl over there, she's never felt any emotions. See if you can make her feel something.* Have I got it right?'

'Almost. But you'd already redlined once before I met you.'

Yes, I had. I remember the flash of red before Sia turned the saw off. 'So the cancelled memrase procedure. That was the architect too?'

Sam shrugs. 'Probably, I mean he knew that Luc being culled was the catalyst for you experiencing emotions. He wouldn't have wanted to erase that memory, or else you probably never would have felt anything ever again.'

'Which is the point of Eridu, Sam,' I say slowly. 'I've done everything that has been asked of me, and this one architect could ruin it all. I should tell the overseers. He's going directly against everything the founders have ordained.'

'Maybe you could. But, Eve, wouldn't the overseers already know? Maybe they're in on it.'

I look at Sam, realisation dawning on me. I don't really care about the overseers, but I did care about him. 'So everything you made me feel,' I say slowly, 'was because it was your job? You wanted me to experience emotions because the architect told you to? And,' I swallow. 'And you never felt anything at all, did you?'

'You can believe whatever you like, Eve, as long as you don't fail the harvest.'

When the words come out of my mouth, I'm pleased to see that my monitor remains blue. 'Oh, don't worry. There's no chance that I am coming to the Grid anytime soon if it means spending time with you.'

Sam nods, and smiles without humour. 'That one's called hate.'

'Goodbye, Sam.'

'It wasn't all a lie, you know.'

I don't want to hear it. I turn and walk out of the door, thankful that I will never have to see him, ever again.

XXXII

Perhaps it was the wrong decision, choosing to *feel* for a few days, but much to my surprise, I find it easier than ever to get back on top of my emotions. I am Alexa, the founder, the god with no feeling. I build up the walls inside me with mortar so thick that nothing can ever seep through, ever again. Each time I start to think of Sam or Luc I clamp down on my feelings tightly and focus on my schoolwork. I pass every academic test with a score of one hundred per cent. I spend long hours in the gym and my emotional control is unparalleled again. I start doing additional volunteer hours as well, just to keep myself busy.

I can't make it back into the top six, of course; it's too late for that. But there are no more redlines, no more amber lines even, and I pour myself into the virtues.

I'm not going to be harvested for a premium occupation, but I have little interest in being an overseer or an architect anyway. If I can keep my emotions under control then maybe, just maybe I can avoid being culled.

I just want to be a preschool teacher. And I just want to forget. If the architect thinks that he's going to jeopardise my harvest scores, then he has another thing coming.

The only testing area which I continue to fall down in is my socialisation score, but the thought of talking to others, of opening myself up to the potential of feeling emotions again is too much to bear. Hana tries to speak with me a few times, but I look right through her, pushing her – pushing everyone – far, far away.

Sitting alone, I move through each day, each week, and each month upholding the virtues. My guardians are pleased with my progress, and so they generally leave me alone as well. By the time we reach the harvest, I'm in thirteenth position. Not amazing, of course, but acceptable; better than I could have hoped for, really, after dropping so close to the bottom. Plenty of people in thirteenth position have succeeded in the harvest, and I am becoming increasingly more confident that I will too.

The cycle ticks slowly forward until we are finally there, the first day of the harvest, the event that I have been in training for throughout my entire life. The one occasion that we all know about, and yet is shrouded in so much uncertainty. I know that there will be tests, and lots of them. There are tests for all the academic subjects, as well as physical tests. I'm not at all concerned about these areas. Some of our harvest scores come from observations over our entire lives, and I can only hope that my short period of indiscretions earlier in the cycle will be cancelled out by seventeen years of being virtuous. Praise the founders.

And if I'm sent to the Grid? I push the thought away. If I am, then there's nothing I can do about it. There's no point in dwelling on things that we can't control.

My guardians sit down with me at breakfast on the morning of the first day of the harvest.

'We have been very pleased with your progress,' says my prime, and I nod.

'Me too.'

'Praise Alexa.'

'Praise Alexa,' I repeat dutifully. 'Prime, how did you find the harvest?'

He thinks for a moment. 'Oh, Eve, it was a long time ago. Time gets a little blurry at the edges.'

I just nod. Perhaps there's some sort of clause when you go through the harvest that says that you can't speak to anyone about it.

There is a beep from my flexi-screen and I peer down at the alert which reminds me to make my way to the auditorium. As if I'd forget.

I farewell my guardians and walk to the institute, taking A-Tunnel of course. I haven't gone the long way since… I push that thought away too.

There is less pomp than I thought there would be when I arrive at the institute. I suppose they are saving that for the harvest ceremony at the end of two days of testing. First, we are funnelled into a variety of classrooms to begin the academic tests. Biology, chemistry, mathematics, history… The tests take up most of the first day, and by the end of it, my brain feels empty, as though all the answers have literally been removed from my mind and transferred into the appropriate spaces on my flexi-screen. I am pleased with my performance, however, and am confident that I did well.

The physical tests take place in the afternoon, and I run faster and lift more than I have in my entire life. Surely I will be harvested, and not culled. Surely. But that's probably what Luc thought at this stage of the harvest, too. Breathe.

We don't return to the multi at the end of the day. Instead, we sleep in a room of temporary pods behind the institute. For the first time, I start to think about life beyond the harvest. Do the caterpillars in the Insectarium think about life beyond the chrysalis, I wonder? Or are they the same as us, putting all of their energy into preparing for the one big event, without ever really thinking about what it's going to be like on the other side? Of course, it's more likely that the caterpillars will eventually spread their wings and leave the cocoon, than it is that we will pass the harvest.

But if I do, then I will leave my guardians and move to Block C, where the harvested adults reside until they are partnered. I climb up into my pod and lie there with the roof open, thinking about my imminent future. A few people are chattering about the day, but most are silent, exhausted. We've ticked off the academic and physical tests, so I'm sure that tomorrow must be the emotional tests. I have never been more prepared.

'Eve?'

I roll onto my side and look over the edge of my pod to see Hana standing there, redlining.

'I mucked up,' she says.

'Shhhh, Hana. Breathe.'

She closes her eyes and after a minute her monitor transitions down to amber, but she can't seem to make it return to blue.

'I'm sure you didn't muck up,' I try to reassure her.

'I did.' Her voice sounds panicked.

'Try not to think about it. Be content, have faith in the tests. Besides, going to the Grid is just a different way of serving Eridu's future.'

Her monitor becomes red again and I sigh.

'What do you think it's going to be like tomorrow?' I ask.

She shrugs. We've heard the rumours, of course. Some say that if your monitor displays so much as a hint of amber throughout the testing then regardless of your academic scores you are automatically culled. That can't be right though, surely.

'It'll be fine,' I say.

She nods and walks away to find her pod, monitor still flashing crimson, so that I am left alone with my thoughts.

XXXIII

When my pod fills with light, it takes me a moment to remember that I'm in the middle of the harvest. I feel like I will just step out of my pod into the multi, preparing for another day at the institute.

'Good morning, Eve,' says my flexi-screen. 'Last night you slept for five hours, twenty-three minutes. Your sleep quality was… excellent. No lifestyle changes recommended.'

I yawn and check the time on my monitor. It is early, far earlier than we are usually woken up. I press the button behind my flexi-screen and my pod cracks open, revealing a room full of yawning, groggy students stumbling out of their pods. In the centre of the swarm of grey stands a single crimson beacon. I recognise his face; it's Architect Nik, the architect who brought Sam back and asked him to… I let the thought trail off. Now is definitely not the time to think about the incident. Perhaps once the harvest is over and my monitor is removed I will allow myself to think of him – and Luc – again. Hell, maybe I'll even activate the transfer program and talk to them. Maybe. But not right now.

It seems counter-intuitive to wake us so early; surely they want us to be at our best for the final test. Or maybe they don't. Perhaps they are so concerned about harvesting the most worthy students that the greater the number of challenges facing us, the better. I give myself a shake, I have faith in the tests.

'Good morning, everyone,' says the architect, and his voice echoes around the large room. 'My name is Nik, and I will be leading you through your final tests. Please get changed quickly, and then line up over here.' He gestures to the side of the room.

I head over to the bathrooms and change into a clean jumpsuit, aware that this will be the final day I will be dressed in grey. Tomorrow, I will be in blue. That, or I will have no use for physical attire anymore.

Returning to the main room, I line up dutifully behind the others. Nobody speaks, perhaps because we are tired, or maybe because we feel the weight of the harvest pressing down upon us.

'Are we all here? Okay, I would like you to come with me,' says the architect. I look at his face, wondering why he has a vendetta against me, why he wants me to fail the harvest. Or perhaps it isn't personal, and he just chose the name at the top of the list to be involved with his sick game.

'Do we get to eat, first?' says a voice from behind me.

I think that whoever said it meant to just say it quietly to a friend, but the question echoes around the large space.

The architect smiles, but it doesn't reach his eyes. 'You can eat when we get back.'

Get back from where? Nobody asks, and we all follow him dutifully along the corridor, turn right, and then we are in the tunnels. We walk quietly along C-tunnel, none of us feeling confident enough to instigate even a whispered conversation. The problem with the tunnels is that our voices can carry. And what would we talk about, anyway? None of us knows where we are going.

I look up at the roof but the paintings of the clouds have been replaced. Instead of clouds, the ceiling is now filled with mottos and lines from the Book of Eridu. *For the greater good; to be content is to be free; sacrifice is necessary for success,* and so on. All traces of the *old world* must have finally disintegrated, flaking off onto the concrete floor. Well, it's about time I suppose.

We turn off at the transfer centre, and I hear the whispers start behind me. 'We can't have all been culled, can we?' Nobody answers. As I enter the doors, I glance sideways, at the little bushes nestled beside the building, but all the berries must have been picked already. What a shame. If I am being culled, I would have liked to taste one of the succulent fruits one last time.

We file dutifully into the centre, and down the corridor towards the chambers. Five at a time, we are directed into the awaiting open doors. There are no explanations forthcoming, and I enter the first small room.

The bed has been pushed against the wall, and five chairs squat expectantly in a semi-circle in the centre of the room.

'Take a seat,' says a voice, and I turn to see a woman in blue standing near the transfer equipment.

I watch myself take a seat, along with the other students. Perhaps I should be protesting, saying that I don't want to be culled, that I will try harder. But where would that leave me? Even if I succeeded in not being transferred, where would I go? There is nowhere to run.

There are no straps on the arms of this chair, at least. In a way, going to the Grid might not be so bad, anyway. If our consciousness really is plucked out of our bodies and sent to the Grid – as I'd like to believe – then Luc will be there. And Gran. I will be able to smile. I will be connected, forever. But what will it be like, existing without substance? Will I simply be floating until my guardians contact me on their flexi-screens? My stomach drops. They won't be contacting me, of course. The memrase procedure will take care of that.

I try to ignore the echoes of my voice, telling Sam that being transferred isn't the eternal life I thought it was. That they are making replicas, not really sending your consciousness to the Grid. I close my eyes and try to imagine that the seat is comforting me, holding me, as I wish Sam was.

Oh for founders' sake, I thought I was beyond all that. I hastily rebuild the walls.

The transfer agent wheels a large trolley of transfer equipment into the centre of the room. There is no sound as it rolls smoothly across the floor. I risk a glance at the other students with me. Their faces are all blank slates, mirroring my own. The agent doesn't introduce herself, but her nametag announces that she is called Tesa. As she attaches the sticky pads to the temples of one of the students, Hana leans across to me.

'It's a test.'

Clever girl, why didn't I think of it before? Of course it's a test. I feel myself relax. After all, we haven't had the emotional test in the harvest yet, so we can't have been culled. The architects are simply playing off our fears of failing the harvest. Thank goodness I've got Hana here to keep me on track. Besides, we are sitting, not lying on a moveable hospital bed, so if they are really transferring us then it doesn't seem ideal. It would be too hard to move our shells once the essence had been drained out.

Tesa attaches the sensors to my temples and I feel nothing. Did all the others figure it out before me too? Am I that critical of the overseers that I can't even work out basic facts?

'Please relax, and open your minds.'

Tesa flicks the switch.

XXXIV

The realisation that something is actually happening almost makes me feel. Almost. After working out that it was all a test, I had presumed that when Tesa flicked the switch that there would just be silence, she would congratulate us on our restraint, and then we would go to the harvest ceremony. Instead, the machine in front of us hums to life, and I feel a tingle through the sensors.

Then I am falling into myself, seeing images of my life rushing up towards me so that I could almost reach out and touch them. It is as though I am in one of the tunnels, but it is standing on end and I am careening through the endless darkness. On either side of me, instead of words from the Book of Eridu, snippets of memories shoot past me. There's Luc as a young boy, comforting me when I tripped over on the concrete. There's Hana, playing with me in the preschool, colouring on the flexi-screens. There's more recent memories, too. As I see the image of Sam and I – sitting in the base of the pod, my lips touching his – I turn away. The time stretches forever, and then condenses into a single second. The final image I see is blurry, and I can't quite make it out. And then two gloved hands plunge into the liquid and pull me forth from the amniotic tub.

I gasp for breath, and then open my eyes, and I'm relieved to see that I'm still sitting in the transfer chamber. After the rush of memories, I almost expected to find myself in the Grid. Tesa removes the transfer equipment and gestures for us to head outside, back into the main room of the transfer centre. There are no explanations, no reassurances that we just passed the last test.

The other four students all stand up with me and we walk out the door.

My stomach is grumbling by the time everyone returns to the main room. There is a certain lightness in the air, as though everyone has worked out the truth; that we have passed the final test. That we have passed the harvest and will soon find out our positions in society.

I wonder what would have happened to me if I felt something during the simulated transfer procedure. Would I have been asked to stay behind? Would my shell still be lying in the chair back in the small room?

Looking around, I can see Lil, Tara and Polee. There's Mat and Ty too. I look for some of the lower-ranked students. But Hana was in the chamber with me, so I know that she is okay. Who else was near the bottom? I try to recall the leaderboard, but the names become blurry beyond the first couple of pages. Regardless, if anyone was culled, it must have been a small number. Have the overseers done it? Have we finally reached a one hundred per cent pass rate in the harvest?

The architect leads us out of the transfer centre, but instead of turning left, as I expected, which would take us back to the institute, breakfast, and the harvest ceremony, he turns right.

Is there more? Haven't we done enough tests by now?

When we turn into H-tunnel the lightness has dissipated, and there is an air of confusion instead. I feel the students drop into a single-file line in the small, dark space. I'm sure that some of them have never been into this disused tunnel, and are feeling slightly disconcerted right now. Hell, I've been in this tunnel plenty of times and even I'm feeling confused. It doesn't lead anywhere, just to the fenced off open space, and then careens back towards the institute. The rocks reach down towards us like hands. The monitors that I can see are all glowing a cool blue.

We stop at the railing, and then the architect does something I don't expect. He unlocks the gate. I suppress the little thrill that threatens to develop inside me. We are going to go through the little secret door.

We all file through the gate and head across the space.

As we get closer I discover that the door is larger than I imagined, and we step through to find ourselves in a long, dark corridor.

'Follow me.'

We walk in single file, the architect opening three separate doors on the way through. The clang as each heavy door shuts behind us reverberates in the space. If the Grid is a real, physical place then it must be up here somewhere. I look left and right, but there are no doors or passages coming off the main tunnel.

The corridor tilts upwards, and the lights on the roof become less frequent. Finally, we stop at a large door that is unlocked electronically. When the door opens, I step through and the darkness envelops me. I can sense that we are in some place much more… open. A large room, perhaps? But no, the ground feels soft underfoot. I crouch down and touch it. It is coarse and sandy, and some sort of plant adorns the ground.

'I think we are...' says Lil, her voice trailing off.

'Outside. On the surface.'

Is this the test, then? To see if we can control our emotions when we are on the surface? Or are we expected to fight off mutated animals, or work out a way to survive the radiation? Or is this just a hallucination generated by the stim, and my body is still sitting in the transfer centre, or back in the pod?

The other students murmur all around me, perhaps asking similar questions, but the architect keeps walking and so we dutifully follow in his footsteps. What else could we do? There are small rustling sounds around us, and I get the sense that there are some sort of large animals just out of sight. Great.

There is a light up ahead, and as we get closer I can make out a large building, a warehouse of some kind. Filing in, a woman at the door hands each of us a cup of water. I gratefully accept it, the walk has made us all thirsty. It feels even darker inside the warehouse, and I find myself touching the wall with one hand, trying not to bump into anyone or anything. Then a spluttering sound starts up, and a single bulb hanging from the ceiling sparks into life. If it's a hallucination then it's certainly a good one.

'As you have no doubt worked out,' begins the architect. 'We are outside Eridu, on the surface. You have been brought up here for a very special reason. For your final test. Please, take a seat.'

I look around in the dim light, and can make out a couple of hay bales and wooden pallets, just like the ones in the farmyard picture books I used to read with Luc. I end up sitting down on the floor, and I can feel dirt and some sort of straw beneath me. Oh for founders' sake, I think it's real.

I breathe deeply, marvelling at the fact that I *can* breathe. I'm on the surface, and I'm actually breathing. I look around, waiting for the hallucination to start. Or perhaps it won't be a hallucination this time, maybe it'll be something real.

'We will be waiting here for a few minutes, and so, as instructed by the original founders, I will tell you all a story.'

I can't decide if sitting in the semi-darkness, listening to the architect is comforting or not. Would I prefer to be in the full light right now, or is the darkness a type of cushion, simulating the pods. I am a foetus, suspended in the amniotic liquid. I will not feel.

'As you all know, many years ago humanity was on the brink

of extinction. War, poverty, and changing environmental climates had killed millions of people, and then the impossible happened. A virus, a man-made pandemic swept through the world, tumbling through the air, injected into the waterways.'

It's a similar spiel to the one told every year at the harvest ceremony, but this time I don't switch off. It seems so much more real, this time, being on the surface. Perhaps we can never truly appreciate the horror of things until we have actually been there.

'96 per cent of the population died almost instantly, and the other four per cent were scattered around a ruined world. Those survivors who were scientifically trained attempted to band together to create a cure. And that's how Eridu was first born, as a research facility to create a vaccine for the virus.'

I look around at the others, but their faces are shrouded in shadows. I haven't learnt anything new and I wonder why the founders stipulated that we needed to be told this. I sip on the cool water and it makes me feel a little better. The little blue monitor lights flash dimly around the room.

'Unfortunately, they didn't have the resources required to conduct many trials, and the founders of our home ultimately failed in their first pursuit. They couldn't seem to create a vaccine. But they did realise something in their studies, something incredibly important, and that was to do with the genetic code. The six founders of Eridu all had a unique gene which seemed to make them resistant to the virus.'

This is new, and I sit up, listening. It doesn't exactly contradict what we have been told, but it certainly adds to it. The story usually ends with the founders being unable to create a vaccine, and instead forming an underground facility, Eridu, where humanity could continue to thrive while we waited, for as long as it took, to be able to return to the surface.

'Well, the founders thought they had figured it out,' the architect continues. 'They would be the mothers and fathers of the future, because they would pass the genetic code onto their offspring. They were clever. They created the incubation cells that we still use today. For the first ten years the founders focused on breeding and raising children with the correct genetic code, but in the tenth year, when they took the children up into the world above, thinking that they would be immune, disaster struck. The shell of every single child that was taken up top died, right here in this warehouse.'

I shiver, and it's not from the cold. I pull my sleeve over my monitor.

I remember what Sam said, reading out of the Book of Eridu. In the first harvest, in Year Ten, nobody had passed. I never imagined that not passing meant dying. I check myself; there is no death in Eridu. It was only their shells that died, and their essences would have been sent to the Grid.

'The founders were distraught. Their plan all along was to remain underground only until the radiation had settled and they had raised enough immune children to begin the world anew. In light of their failures, they wondered if they had misunderstood the nature of their immunity to the virus. They thought that perhaps they would be the last of humankind, the final six to ever walk the surface of the earth.'

The hay bale prickles my arms and I move slightly, trying to get comfortable. My mind is straying to places that I don't want it to. Images of young children sitting on the ground in front of me overtake my thoughts. One of them looks like Tali.

'The founders were growing older. Ten years of wasted experiments would have been disheartening to anyone. But then they came up with a new theory. Perhaps it wasn't enough for the children to simply have the correct gene, but they also needed to experience precise environmental factors to activate it, to make them immune. The founders toyed with a few ideas. Food, drugs, toxins in the air, pain, radiation; these were all potential factors that could activate the gene. They conducted experiment after experiment, hoping to stumble across the answer.'

The cold in the warehouse permeates my skin and enters my blood. Icy shards pump around my body, and I wonder about my own fate.

'The main problem was that there was no way to tell if the gene had been activated, and the child was immune, except to expose them to the virus. They didn't want to taint Eridu, and so they brought the children up here, at various ages, trying to work out how to save humankind.'

I don't want to hear anymore. I feel sick.

'We know from their notes that it was Alexa who first discovered the link between emotional suppression and activating the gene. Alexa hypothesised that they would need to teach the children to suppress their emotions in order to make them immune. But of course, it's easier said than done.' He hesitates and gazes around the room. I do the same, but everyone is sitting silently, as though frozen in place.

'And so the founders set up the six virtues,' he continues, 'in order to maintain a harmonious society, and they taught everyone to suppress their emotions. The next round of tests were much more successful. The children who were able to effectively suppress their emotions were much more likely to be immune to the virus.'

Praise the founders. So we are immune? Are we finally going to be repopulating the surface? It's too dark to see most of the faces around me, but I can see their monitors glowing blue. It might not be true, I remind myself. The architect might be telling us the most awful story possible, just to try to make us feel, to see who has instilled the virtues.

'There seemed to be a few aspects for success,' he continues. 'First, the children needed to have the correct genetic marker. This marker needed to be activated, and they had to have gone through puberty. The founders worked hard to make sure the system was successful. Four of them returned to the surface to try to grow crops and create resources, but despite being immune to the virus, the radiation was still too strong, and so they concentrated on creating the required resources underground. Besides, they knew the children would die if they walked on the surface before the immunity gene had been activated, so there seemed no point in wasting time and energy on reclaiming the surface.'

It can't be true, I decide. It's just a story to make us feel. After all, if suppressing emotions was necessary for becoming immune to the virus, then surely the overseers would tell us earlier. There would be no need for secrecy.

'Not everyone was able to suppress their emotions, of course; as you know, it is a difficult thing to do. And, when they were brought up to this warehouse on harvest day, they either lived, in which case they went on to continue the future of Eridu, or they did not. Please finish your water and place your cup on the ground.'

We all dutifully do as he asks. The water is hard to swallow. I can feel the coolness as it slides down my throat, and it reminds me of the river in the tunnel that day, not so long ago.

'To this day, we continue the tradition set out by the founders. During the harvest, you complete a range of academic, physical, and behavioural tests to work out where you would be best aligned in Eridu. And then we bring you up here to undertake the most important test of all.' My mind is struggling to comprehend all that he is saying. The ground feels too solid beneath my legs.

'Some of you will be feeling a little ill right now. Don't be concerned. You have been breathing air contaminated with the virus since arriving above ground, and the water you drank is from the nearby stream.' I feel myself breathing faster and I look around at the others. I can't tell which ones are feeling ill and which ones aren't. I know that I feel sick in the stomach, but is that from the virus or from the architect's story? Is this just a hallucination? If so, I have to applaud the architects for creating something so realistic and terrifying. Even I am struggling to stay blue.

'In a moment, some of you are going to leave this warehouse. I am going to ask you to stand, and if you are able to do so then you have passed, you are immune and you will soon be allocated your place in society. Some of you will not succeed. Perhaps you didn't work hard enough to suppress your emotions, and so the gene was never activated. The virus works quickly, first impacting on the brain's ability to manoeuvre peripheral body parts like legs and arms.'

Experimentally, I flex my fingers. Are they hard to bend because they are numb from the cold or because the virus is already affecting me?

'For those left behind, Dixi here can help quicken the process along, if you like.' The architect gestures towards the woman who passed us all the cups of water. 'Since you aren't immune, your shells will be destroyed, becoming fertiliser for the vertical gardens. Do not be afraid, however. Your essences will still travel to the Grid. Earlier, we made copies of your neurological patterns, ensuring that your guardians will be able to contact you once you reach the Grid. Praise Alexa.'

Nobody tries to repeat the familiar saying.

'There is no need for concern,' he reiterates. 'If you cannot stand, then be content with the fact that it is simply your shells that are dying, not your consciousness. Not your true selves.'

Does he think this is comforting?

'As soon as your shell passes away, your consciousness will go to the Grid. Praise progress. Now, follow me.'

The architect turns and walks out the door. I try to repeat the familiar phrase but the words stick in my throat. For founders' sake, am I going to die here on the floor of this warehouse? I correct my thoughts. It's just my shell, after all. I am content.

Some of the students are getting to their feet. Lil. Mat. Tara. I am almost too scared to try, and then I push my hands down onto the ground and stand up. I wobble slightly, but I seem to have my wits about me. I start to follow the others out the door, but then I glance back and see Hana sitting still, leaning against a hay bale.

'Hana, you have to get up now.'

She looks up at me but doesn't move. I walk shakily over to her, and then I notice the others, still sitting down. They are silent. 'Hana, come on.' I take her by the hand but it is cold and unresisting. I try to pull her to her feet, but overbalance and end up making us both fall to the floor. 'Come on, Hana,' I say, but she looks at me, and then moves one finger up into the air. It's a wave. Her lips twitch slightly and I lean in to hear what she is saying.

Her voice is both soft and hoarse, and I can just make out what she is saying. 'Will you talk to me once I've transferred? I don't want to be alone in the Grid.'

This is no hallucination. My heart thunders in my chest.

I nod. 'Of course I will.' Is this a lie? And then I stumble out

of the warehouse and take big gulping breaths of contaminated
air into my lungs.

XXXV

'Congratulations,' says the architect, once those who are able to are assembled back outside the warehouse. There is no doubt in my mind now that this is real.

Everyone on the top couple of pages of the leaderboard seems to be here, and a few from lower down as well who must have had just enough emotional control to activate the gene for immunity. I try to tell myself that it's nice to finally have a full understanding of the founders' plans, but to be honest, the sensation of trying to pick up Hana's weak body is still too fresh in my mind. I feel sick.

'Here we are,' continues the architect. 'Welcome to the future of Eridu. You are all academically superior, physically fit, virtuous, and most importantly, immune to the virus. Follow me.'

Some of the monitors on the wrists of the students around me are flashing amber, but I suppose it doesn't matter now. There is nothing else we can do, so we fall into step behind the architect, and he leads us around the side of the warehouse until we see a smaller, newer building squatting near the warehouse wall.

'Line up, everyone. Your monitors and stims will be removed, and then we will head back into Eridu for the harvest ceremony and your positions for the future. It's over.'

We silently line up and I fall into place behind Lil out of habit. I wonder if she will still look through me, even though the rankings don't matter anymore, but her eyes seem to gaze through everything, not just through me. The first few people enter the building. The warehouse behind me is silent, and I try not to think of what is happening in there right now. After all, there is no point being concerned about things that you cannot control. To be content is to be free.

The line moves quickly, and I hardly have time to think before Lil is swallowed up by the door in front of me. I half-wonder if there was some medicine in the water we were given, or if the numbness is just my brain's reaction to news that it can't quite seem to process.

The students who went in first are starting to emerge from the building now, rubbing their wrists and the skin behind their ears. That will be me, in a moment. How will it feel to have no monitor or stim? To know that I am immune to the virus, and that I can help to rebuild the world on the surface.

But there's more than just the virus to be concerned about, isn't there. There's the darkness, and the radiation too. I think of the sensation of large animals moving around me on the path to the warehouse – if they can survive up here, then I suppose that humans can too.

As I reach the door, I see the architect standing off to the right, and, making up my mind, I step out of line instead.

'Excuse me,' I begin, as I walk towards him.

'Ah, Eve. I'm so pleased to see you.'

Is he, though? Or is he currently adding up how many oxy-creds he lost to the other architects now that I've passed the harvest?

I passed. I don't try to stifle the feeling of triumph, but it is mingled with something else. Guilt, perhaps. Oh, Hana.

'I don't understand,' I begin, and the architect interrupts me.

'It might take a while to process everything.'

'No,' I say, firmly, because I understand everything he told us

in the warehouse about genes and emotions and viruses. What I
don't understand is about Luc.

'Why was Luc culled?'

The architect looks at me for a moment, as though making up
his mind whether to tell me the truth or not.

'Ah, yes,' he says at last, quietly. 'You and your brother were
always so promising. I have been watching you closely since the
beginning.'

He hasn't answered my question, but I just wait, determined
not to go any further until I have some answers.

'I am so pleased to see that you are immune after all, Eve. I
had my doubts – everyone had their doubts – after what happened
to your brother.'

I keep my face blank.

'But my little experiment paid off in the end, didn't it. The
overseers will be so surprised.' It's almost like he is talking to
himself, and not to me at all.

'Experiment?' I say carefully. 'What do you mean?'

The architect glances at the line slowly funnelling into the
building, and then moves away, gesturing for me to follow him.
We don't go far, just along the side of the building a little further,
but I find myself feeling nervous to be alone with him.

'You are special, Eve,' he says quietly. 'Different.'

'Because I was good at controlling my emotions?'

He shakes his head. 'Not just that. You see, from your very
conception you were different than the others.'

This is not what I expected to hear.

'Neither you nor your brother were created out of the frozen
sperm and eggs from the original founders as everyone else here
was.'

He looks at me, as though I should have worked out what he

is hinting at. He seems almost excited, but of course, he can't be. I think hard, and then I work it out. 'What, do you mean I was born naturally? Were my guardians really my mother and father?' I try to sort out how I feel about this.

'Oh no, Eve, not quite. My dear friend – your prime – and I thought that we would try something a bit different. Harvest results weren't improving, you see. The number of immune in each cycle had plateaued. We needed a different solution if we ever hoped to have enough immune adults to rebuild the world.'

I wait, wondering what revelation he is about to uncover. My primary guardian works as a geneticist, so I think that perhaps my genes had been altered in the foetal stage. Maybe that's why suppression of emotions came so easily; I was genetically engineered not to feel. Is this the future of the world? Genetically engineered humans who can't feel, so they are automatically immune? But I had felt emotions, hadn't I. The architect had made sure of that.

'Your brother was the first in Eridu,' says the architect, 'to be cloned.'

I feel the hairs on the backs of my arms stand up.

'His genetic material came from a founder named Elijah. You probably don't know much about him, unless you've read the Book of Eridu. He was so promising, and your guardians were doing so well, so we cloned another.'

I don't need him to tell me, I already know.

'Alexa.'

'Yes.'

My heart thumps in my chest and pushes my cloned blood cells around my veins. I feel sick.

'Your brother was always so good at the tests. So good at suppressing emotions; it's like he never even felt them to begin with. We thought for sure that he would come up here during the harvest and walk right back out of it. And if he did, well, perhaps we could create an entire city out of clones. An immunity rate of one hundred per cent. We could move to the surface far sooner than we hoped and reclaim our rightful place in the world.'

'But he didn't,' I say, and my voice comes out steadier than I thought it would.

'No,' agrees Architect Nik. 'He didn't.'

I imagine Luc coming up here on the day of the harvest and sitting in the warehouse opposite me. I quickly shut these thoughts down.

'We were adamant,' says Nik, 'that the gene would have been activated. But we are learning all the time, you see. The other architects thought the problem with Luc was that he was a clone, and that's why the gene was never expressed. They said that I should never have begun the experiments. They were certain that there was no hope for you either, or for any of the other handful of students younger than you who are also clones of the founders. According to them, some aspect of the cloning procedure must have interfered with gene activation.'

'Great, so you brought me up here, expecting me to die?'

'Oh no, Eve. Nobody dies in Eridu.'

I think of our little trip to the transfer centre. 'Okay, but my physical body. You thought it would be affected by the virus.'

'The others did,' he says, simply. 'Not me. See, I thought there may have been a different reason for Luc failing at the harvest. He was the best student we ever had, you see...'

His voice trails off and I wonder if somewhere within his perfectly controlled outer shell there is a hint of sadness or regret.

'I had this hypothesis that Luc had been too good. We always thought that just suppressing emotions was enough, but then I thought, what if Luc's immunity gene had never activated because it had never undergone the stress situations necessary for transformation. If you never feel the emotions at all then the genes are never activated.'

I start putting it all together. 'So you got Sam to make me feel emotions so that the gene would be activated? You were trying to help me?'

'Oh, you know about my little deal with Sam do you?'

I nod, and the architect looks pleased. 'We all realised that you would likely go the same way as your brother. That when you were exposed to the virus, your shell would die within a few minutes like his did. So I took… measures… to try to counteract that. The overseers thought it was ridiculous, but when I organised for the boy to play his role in the experiment, there was little they could do to stop what was already in motion.'

I lean against the building, listening to the muffled voices coming through the boards. Wooden boards, made from trees. 'Sam's not from the Grid, is he?'

The architect gazes at me for a long moment. 'No,' he says at last. 'I thought if you believed that Luc could come back, then you would feel hope. I wanted – needed – you to feel all of the emotions, Eve. And then I wanted you to suppress them. I couldn't handle another one of my clones perishing on the floor of a dusty warehouse.'

One of *his* clones. I feel my identity fly away in the slight breeze playing across my face.

'Where is he now?'

'Luc? He's in the Grid, just like you have been told. We can't bring people back though, why would we bother? The ones who have been culled were unworthy.'

I want to scream at the architect, to tell him that Luc *was* worthy and that I'm not interested in being his experiment. But I just keep my voice even and my monitor hidden.

'No, I mean, where's Sam?'

'Oh, Eve, that doesn't matter, does it?'

Do I hear a note of pity in his voice? Sympathy for the clone who couldn't feel emotions and then when she did, it all fell apart.

I suppose it doesn't matter, really, and yet I do want to know – so I just wait, silently.

'Sam lives with a group of other survivors – and I use that term loosely – in a containment facility, 100 kilometres or so that way,' Nik waves vaguely off to his right. 'We trade services fairly regularly with his uncle.'

I nod, feeling like I've felt so many emotions in the past few minutes that I'm not even sure how to react to this information.

'Do you know if Sam is…?'

'Immune?' Nik shakes his head. 'No. He doesn't have the correct genetic marker. We checked. We check everyone that we come into contact with up here.'

'So he's a *mask*?'

'Well, yes, he would have had to wear an oxygen mask to travel between here and the containment facility.' Nik glances across at the line of students, which has dwindled down to almost nothing. 'Eve, we are nearly ready to go back to Eridu. Go and get your monitor and stim removed.'

I turn back towards the building, and then I notice something that makes me go cold. On the back of the head of the student standing nearest to me is a small bald patch.

'Why did you bother telling us all of that if you are just going to erase our memories?' My voice is icy.

The architect follows my gaze. 'Oh, Eve, it's not a mandatory procedure. It's a choice.'

Is it a choice that I, too, will make when I get my monitor and stim removed? Or do I want to return to Eridu with the knowledge of what we have all sacrificed in order to continue the human race, fresh in my mind?

No, surely it's better this way. Perhaps I'll even ask them to remove the knowledge that I'm a clone of Alexa.

I no longer know who I am.

Did I ever know who I was?

I take a step towards the building, trying to be content with the fact that in a few minutes' time I won't need to know about any of this. I hesitate, and then turn back towards the architect.

'No.'

The edge of the sky is lighter now, and there is a brilliant orange where the darkness touches the ground. It is like the amber on the monitors, but brighter, more intense.

'No? You don't want to remove the monitor? The stim? Suit yourself.' He turns away from me, clearly planning on ushering the rest of the immune along the path back to Eridu.

'No,' I repeat, louder this time. 'I'm not coming back to Eridu.'

I feel sick as I say it. Do I really mean it, though? The architect's face is no longer blank when he turns back towards me, but I can't figure out what the expression is.

'You want to stay up here? Eve, you can survive the virus, but what about everything else?'

I shrug, and I know I should go with him, but my feet refuse to move.

'Eve, what are you doing?'

I look across the desert in the direction of the containment facility.

'How long does it take to walk 100 kilometres?'

'Don't be stupid. You'll never make it. And remember, he

never actually cared for you. It was all part of his job.'

Nik reaches out towards me, and then my feet work again, and I step out of his way.

'Look,' says the architect, 'come back with me. Come to the ceremony. Nobody knows what they are being harvested for yet, but I may as well tell you. You are going to be an overseer, Eve. That means that you get some say in how we move forward. We just do what we think is best to save humanity, in the vision of the founders.'

Is he trying to convince me or himself?

'If you don't like it, then being an overseer is the perfect position for you. You will live out your life peacefully, making decisions that affect the future of humanity. And when the time comes, you will transfer. There will never be war, or violence, or sickness in there.'

He reaches out his hand and I desperately want to take it.

'You're right,' I begin. 'Growing up in Eridu, I was safe. There is no crime, no hunger, and no illness. Everyone has their place.'

He smiles at me, encouraged. 'Come on, your guardians will be looking forward to seeing you on that stage.'

'There is no idleness in Eridu,' I continue. 'No greed. But there's also no companionship. No love. No disappointment, but no excitement either.'

He stares at me. 'For a clone of Alexa, you sound nothing like her.' His voice is flat. 'If you don't come with me, then everyone will think you have been culled. Are you that selfish, to make your guardians, your friends, believe that?'

I shrug. 'I've realised a few things recently. The only person I could truly call my friend, who saw beyond my ranking, is lying on the floor of that warehouse. And you know what? Your perfect system put a stop to that. Besides, I'm sure you will be offering my guardians the memrase procedure soon enough.'

'There's no other way, you know,' he says quietly. 'This is just how it has to be.'

Is it, though?

'We've tried different options, over the years, but the current system is what seems to produce the most immune adults. And Eve, if we want to one day repopulate the world, then we *do* need immune adults. And not just any immune adults, but those who are going to rebuild society in the proper way.'

I don't know what I feel. I need time, but the horizon is on fire and my monitor is crimson. I gaze at the warehouse, where the woman who gave us the drink is dragging a trolley out of the double doors. I turn away from the silhouette of overflowing limbs.

'They aren't dead, you know,' says Nik.

'I know.'

'The shells aren't them.'

I nod and gaze off into the distance across the flat, sandy ground.

'If you stay up here, there's no guarantee that you will go to the Grid one day. That privilege is reserved for those in Eridu.'

The world is burning and I feel a thrill of fear. It's the sun, which means the darkness must be over. I wonder what else the overseers have lied to us about.

'I'm leaving now, Eve,' says the architect. 'With you or without you.'

I don't answer him.

'So what, you are going to throw your life away for love? For a false love built on lies?'

'No, I'm not throwing my life away for love,' I say, and he relaxes. 'That would be foolish.'

I look him in the eye. 'I'm throwing it away so that I can *live*.'

And with that, I turn and walk in the direction of the rising sun.

———————————

Thank you for reading! If you enjoyed this book, please consider leaving a review.

ALSO BY ALANAH ANDREWS

Eridu Series
The Harvest (FREE novella – go to www.alanahandrews.com)
Eve of Eridu
Culled (Coming 2019)

The Mutation Chronicles
Exiles

Short Stories
The King Experience (Finalist in the Roswell Award – go to www.alanahandrews.com to read for free)

Beyond: A Short Story Collection
Vessels (On the Brink, *Windswept Writing*, 2019)
Edge (Beginnings, *Deadset Press*, 2018)
Earth II (A Flash of Words, *Scout Media*, 2018)
The Call (Utopia: Pending, *Fallacious Rose*, 2018)
Transference (Eternal, *Hammond House*, 2018)
Cleanaway 3000 (Zonal Horizons, *Audio Arcadia* 2018)

http://www.alanahandrews.com

ABOUT THE AUTHOR

Alanah Andrews is an English teacher in Victoria, Australia. She lives with her husband, kids, a lizard, husky, and pony. She dreams of being a gypsy and travelling Australia in a bus.

www.facebook.com/alanahandrewsauthor
www.twitter.com/alanah_writes
www.alanahandrews.com